The Tales of Northborough

RENEE KENNY

First published in 2018 by
PANORMI BOOKS

The Tales of Northborough

ISBN 978-99957-1-333-1 paperback edition.
ISBN 978-99957-1-334-8 ebook edition.

Published by
PANORMI BOOKS
panormibooks.com

Printed in the United States of America.

Dedication

To my family

Acknowledgments

I would like to thank my editor, Marcelle, for putting all this together and wanting to tell my stories.

Thank you to my parents for letting me read for untold hours in my room, something I still do.

Thank you to my family. You make every day worthwhile and I am so happy that you are part of my life.

Contents

The Tales of Northborough

Book One

THE ENCHANTED CUP

Chapter One

Before the last Druids had left Albion, in the reign of King Malcolm, or Good King Malcolm as he was known, there lived a boy, Ranaulf, together with his mother and father, in the forest of Northborough. Ranaulf's mother feared one thing above all else. More than fire, disease, hunger, or the ruffians who roamed the forest, she feared the pewter cup that rested upon her mantelpiece. It was the only thing of value the family owned – and had owned – across the centuries, being handed down to the eldest daughter in every generation. Thus she kept it, but out of her young son's reach.

The cup was fascinating to little Ranaulf. It was the one piece of finery in a home of rough-hewn goods and furniture. It was shaped like a castle turret. Little arrow-slits wound up the sides. The arched, horned tail of a devilish dragon formed its handle. It was nothing like the hollowed-out, wooden cups that were used at their board every day.

"You are *not* to drink from this cup!" his mother warned. *"No, no, no!"*

Although he was too young to understand her warning, Ranaulf knew the word "no" and that the cup was a forbidden toy. He could not possibly comprehend that to drink from it would transport him to another place and that the place could be a mountain, a field, a ship at sea, or a busy village shop. He would be separated from those who loved him: his mother, Matilda, and his father, Hugh, until he again drank from the cup.

11

Ranaulf's mother told him stories as she sat by the fire, holding him upon her lap, twirling locks of his golden hair around her finger. Matilda related stories of great-great uncle Gregory, who had drunk a draught from the cup on a dare and disintegrated into a bubbly brew that spilled on the ground. And great-great-great grandmother Margotta, who, it was told, had stolen the cup from the Druids, only to drink of it and fly out of the window of a church, never to be seen again.

But this strange cup held an inexplicable fascination to all who gazed upon its mysterious craftsmanship. In what century had it been formed? Had it always rested upon this isle or had it traveled the seas from distant shores? Could it bring wealth or happiness to its owner, or was the one who possessed it destined to suffer tragedy?

Turning the cup so that she held it in her left hand, she looked upon the face of the dragon. This was the back, the side of the cup which usually faced the wall. But now, Matilda looked upon the evil, bloodthirsty visage of the beast. The creature locked its gray, lifeless eyes with those of the woman and she set the cup, handle to the right, upon the mantel in its usual pose.

Chapter Two

Years passed and, as an answer to Matilda's prayers, the mysterious cup sat like a spider in the corner of a barn, doing no more harm than gathering cobwebs and dust.

One sunny day, Ranaulf sat near the fireplace, soaking in its warmth and playing with the little wooden soldiers his father had carved for him. Ranaulf was fair-haired, with a cherubic face and aqua-blue eyes. He was a well-fed lad, with plenty of extra tissue to last him through the difficult

Northborough winters. He wore a slightly-soiled tunic and leather sandals on this early spring morning.

The boy looked up at the unusual cup on the mantel, understanding that it was the one thing in the house that he was not to touch. But Ranaulf's armies were upset by his cats, Cullin and Oisin, racing in from outdoors. Both cats were as black as the necks of geese, but Cullin had a small patch of sand-colored fur under his eye. That is how the young lad told them apart. Oisin ran right through the soldiers, teasing Cullin by pausing just long enough to fool the latter into a useless pounce. The next moment, Oisin jumped up on the mantel, followed by Cullin. Oisin's tail brushed the cup and down it tumbled, landing right in the boy's lap.

Ranaulf was at first shocked, but then became delighted with his cats for presenting him with the curious vessel he had just known from afar. He toddled around the humble cottage, looking for his mother to show her his new treasure, but she was in the kitchen garden, preparing the soil for the spring planting. Matilda concentrated on her work, bent over the plot, picking out the rocks and digging up the soil. *This is a cup,* thought Ranaulf. *Now, I have touched it and no harm has come to me.* So, in a clumsy manner, he poured himself a drink from the water jug and took a sip.

In a flash, Ranaulf felt strange, as though he were turning inside out. He closed his eyes, dizzy and spinning, traveling without moving; faster and faster. He cried out, but his voice seemed to wrap around the air like a tornado and fall into the void. The cup fell from his chubby hands onto the floor and landed with the face of the dragon staring up at the ceiling.

Chapter Three

Matilda washed the dirt from her hands and walked into the cottage, drying them on her once-white apron. She tucked a few wisps of hair behind her ears.

"Ranaulf," she called, "where are you, son?"

It was unusual for Ranaulf not to toddle, as best he could, up to his mother whenever he heard her enter the house. But Maltilda stopped short when she approached the hearth. There, on the floor amidst the rushes and toy soldiers, lay the cup. She knew right away what had happened. Her son was gone -- GONE -- and she might never see him again! He had been taken from her by the evil magic in the cup.

"Why did I take a chance?" she lamented. "Why did I allow the cup to be left on the mantel? How could I have ignored the ancient curse? Was my son not worth more to me than a thousand pewter cups?"

These thoughts tormented Matilda and she wailed all the louder for blaming herself. Her husband, hearing her sobbing, came running to the cottage. He too knew what had occurred when he saw the cursed cup on the floor. Hugh tried to put his arm around Maud, as he called her, but she had picked the cup up and started to run. She was running along the path to the sea, barefooted and bare-headed in the springtime sun. Her braids fought against their ribbons until they untied and flew behind her like pennons above a castle on a windy morn.

Matilda ran and ran, breathing heavily, looking straight ahead, pushing her legs to keep going, although they were as weak as reeds of grass. At last, she reached the path's end at the edge of a rocky cliff overlooking the Narrow Sea. With every ounce of strength left in her weary body, she heaved the enchanted cup into the whirling green sea below. Then Matilda fell to her knees, to the ground, with great tears of despair falling from her eyes.

"My baby, my Ranaulf! My baby, my Ranaulf," she repeated.

Hugh, who had followed her, also cried for he had loved the boy more than life itself.

After a while, he said, "Come, Maud, let us go home. The sun sinks on the horizon."

"No, Hugh, I cannot return to that place. I will think of my little one – where he sat at the board, where he slept in his bed, where he played on the hearth. Let us move away from this place and its memories, otherwise I fear that I shall sink deep within its sorrow."

"It will be as you say, wife," answered gentle Hugh.

Chapter Four

When he opened his eyes, Ranaulf was in a strange place. A peasant boy, he sat on the nursery floor in a king's castle. The magic in the cup had taken him to Caradon Hall, home of King Malcolm, Queen Aurelia, their two daughters, nurses, ladies-in-waiting, pages, squires, smiths, knights, stewards, cooks, falconers, masters of the hounds, barbers, and all the others necessary to maintain a royal residence.

He was discovered by the nurses of the princesses. The women were puzzled by his appearance, but fell in love with the boy with yellow hair and azure eyes. He had such a gentle disposition that the nurses came to fighting over his care. Ranaulf did not forget his parents, but was, at the moment, enjoying all he attention and fuss that was paid to him.

He had landed upon his bottom; his chubby legs splayed out at a ninety-degree angle in front of him. There were *oooh's* and *aaah's* as nurses and ladies-in-waiting came running to see if he were hurt. It *had* hurt a little, the bump; the landing. But that did not matter, did it?

The question was, where was his mother and why were all these strange women simpering over him?

Ranaulf began to wail, "Maamaaa, Maamaa," his voice trailing off as he was shushed by a maiden.

Her gowns were lovely, tied with silken rope around the waist, but with wide gossamer sleeves hanging from the wrist. The skirts were full of flowing movement and the overall effect was one of grace and poise.

Ranaulf recalled his own mother, Maud. She had worn the simple kirtle of a peasant wife. It bore no adornments – no jewels nor golden ropes; no embroidery brightened the shapeless dress. But that face, the face of his mother, it was dear to him like nothing else in the world. He wanted her and began to shake as he fought off more tears. Against his will and the hush, hushing of the maidens, the drops welled up inside his eyes and fell upon his tunic.

"There, there, now, laddie," a diminutive woman with deep brown eyes that crinkled up at the edges told him. "Your mama's not here at the moment, but we will take good care o'ye."

Ranaulf looked up to the nurse, who had taken a gamble by saying those words for, as she said them, a most breathtaking woman descended the stairs. The boy could not believe his eyes. She was beautiful, with a regal calmness that covered everyone in the room like a cloak on a wet day. The nurse hoped that the woman would agree to keep the forlorn little lad on at the castle. She held her breath.

"Your majesty," the ladies said in unison, all curtsying low, touching the floor and bowing their heads.

The woman, who wore a golden circlet about her hair, which was the color of summer-ripe wheat, asked them to rise. Ranaulf still sat on the floor, sniffling and heaving.

Now it was quiet, except for the little sounds from the new arrival. Queen Aurelia walked up to Ranaulf and knelt down before him, then sat back upon her heels. She touched his cleft chin with her gloved hand. The boy looked up. Their gaze met and the lad glanced down again. He was afraid of this great lady.

The queen was thinking that fortune had smiled upon her. Here was a boy, a toddler only, whom she could love as her own because she had no sons. He had been poor, she could see that, but it was clear that he was strong and well-fed. She remembered her position and resisted the urge to cry.

Queen Aurelia gathered the child in her arms and held him until his heaves became mere sighs. She stroked his marvelous yellow curls, then kissed him softly upon the forehead. Ranaulf was no longer afraid.

"Nurses, ladies," she spoke. "I do not know from whence this child came, but I do know that he has appeared here for a reason. That reason I know not, but we shall know it one day. The child," as she stooped low to look at him in the face and gently whispered a question to him, to which he responded, "the child, Ranaulf, is to be raised as though he were the son of King Malcolm. See that it be done."

And one last time, she bent low to the boy, kissed him and said, "Be not afraid."

Then the queen gathered her many skirts and walked away from the nursery. Her perfectly oval face, her serene eyes round to the point of astonishment; her hair smooth, straight and reflecting light like a newly-polished chalice, everything about her spoke of majesty. But inside the queen, her emotions tangled as she knew not for what purpose this magic had been visited upon her castle. *Was it a portent of good or evil?*

Her back straight, her eyes fixed ahead, Queen Aurelia ascended the stairs from the nursery, thinking of the strange event that had just occurred.

"I must banish worry from my head," she told herself. "The child is a *gift* from the fates. His presence can only be for the good of our family and for the good of Northborough."

And secure in her knowledge that the nurses would give him the best care possible, she walked toward the solar in search of her husband, King Malcolm, to tell him the news.

Chapter Five

Ranaulf grew in knowledge and stature, a tall boy, blessed with good health and a quick mind. He lost his chubbiness as he gained in height. He took his lessons with the princesses. The children played together.

When the lad became old enough to learn the chivalrous arts, he became a page and was given a small room of his own in the castle. While it was customary to send boys away to relatives for their training, Ranaulf already resided with folk not his own, so he remained at Caradon Hall. He learned swordsmanship and archery. He began his duties in the stables and at the board. He fed and groomed the horses; he made certain that their tack was in good repair. Mealtimes he stood behind the squires, filling their goblets with wine or adding a leg of mutton to their plates.

Ranaulf had grown into the handsomest of boys. However, although all in the castle treated him with kindness, he remained painfully aware of his humble beginnings. He was still an orphan and but for the generosity of the king and queen, he would have been assigned the meanest, dirtiest chores in the palace.

At this time, he began to miss his parents terribly. Images from the distant past began to trouble his dreams. Where was his mother, who sang softly as she put him to bed each night? Where was his father, who took him on grand walks in the forest; carrying him home upon his great, mountain-like shoulders when the lad was too weary to walk? Where was his home, Cullin and Oisin, his dogs, his forest?

Ranaulf now realized that he had done wrong by drinking from the cup and he knew that the only way to get home again was to find it – and drink from it once more.

Chapter Six

Ranaulf got a chance to find the cup a few years later. He was now a squire and owned his own horse. He had learned hunting and falconry. He had practiced jousting with a blunted spear and shooting with the long bow. He was expected to write romantic verse, but tore up each sheet of parchment in disgust.

"I will never be any good at this," he lamented.

Danish pirates had been capturing the ships of Northborough and taking their goods. King Malcolm wanted to start a marine defense force to protect his merchant ships. Ranaulf got word of this endeavor and asked the king to permit him to go.

King Malcolm was reluctant to let the young boy leave on so dangerous a mission, but knew that his adopted son would need to have adventures to become a knight. Thus he allowed the lad to travel to the windswept shore where he boarded the ship, the *Cormorant.*

Ranaulf approached the dock to find the *Cormorant* rocking gently in the tame surf. The sky, forget-me-not blue, held tousled clouds like sheep's wool. Ranaulf took a deep breath of the fish-scented air. White gulls overhead shrieked and dove for food.

Perhaps I shall have my adventure soon, he thought as he climbed up to the deck. He was met by the ship's mate. A man with an amiable face reached out to shake Ranaulf's hand.

"So you've arrived. Come from his majesty, the king, have you? We've been waiting for you, lad," he said, smiling under his big, unruly moustache.

Ranaulf noticed a wide sword cut across the man's cheek. The old salt's auburn eyebrows were so bushy that his eyes had to squint to see past them, yet he seemed kind.

"I am under the king's command to assist in any way that I can to pursue the brigands who plunder our merchant vessels."

"I am called John and I am pleased to make your acquaintance."

"Squire Ranaulf is my name. I am glad to meet you, John. This is my first voyage."

"Do not worry about anything. Captain Brendan is as fine a mariner as you will ever see. Take your bag and let's go to his cabin where I will introduce you."

Chapter Seven

John led Ranaulf to the small room that served as the captain's quarters. Captain Brendan was bent over a map.

Ranaulf noticed that the man's dark, wavy hair fall against his coarse and wool-knit sweater.

"Captain, this is our new hand, Squire Ranaulf."

The captain stood up and shook the lad's hand. As he did, their eyes met. The newcomer was transfixed by the power of the mariner's gaze. Brendan seemed to look through Ranaulf's eyes into his very soul. Ranaulf could not stop looking at Brendan's eyes. *Sea-green,* he thought, *and like the sea, turbulent; violent.*

The boy had never seen such eyes, they made him nervous. It was almost as if these eyes were alive separately, that they were made of the sea itself and moved and lived within it. But the captain's handsome face was calm and peaceful. The man put his arm around Ranauf and led the new hand to an oaken table black with age.

"Sit down," he bid Ranaulf. "Are you hungry, lad?"

Those were the words Ranaulf had most desired to hear. The three sailors sat down to a simple meal of bread, cheese, and wine. The wine warmed Ranaulf and made him sleepy, so he was shown his bunk and thus ended his first day aboard ship.

Day after day, the *Cormorant* and her crew patrolled Albion's coast. They escorted several merchant vessels across the Narrow Sea. They even had an encounter with a Norse pirate ship. Ranaulf wanted to make war against them.

"My arrows will pierce their thieving chests!" he exclaimed.

"Nay, nay, lad, you are needed to take John's place at the helm. Hold her steady and I'll be grateful. You are young. You will have many chances for battle in the years ahead."

Ranaulf knew he had to obey. He admired the captain and did not want to disappoint him, yet like all young men, he was impatient to prove his worth. He wanted to become a knight; he wanted to be known for his bravery and good deeds. Ranaulf watched Brendan ascend the stairs to the deck.

"One day, I will make you proud of me," he whispered behind the man's back.

Chapter Eight

The days blended together on the open sea, so that the young man knew not Monday from Thursday. They docked frequently for supplies, so their food was always fresh. He was proud of their ship, knowing that she helped the Northborough trade by the mere presence of her pennants flapping in the salty breeze. Pirates came to fear her, knowing the deadly aim of the experienced bowmen aboard.

Once, a pirate ship surrendered to the captain and they brought her crew ashore to be tried in court. The pirate ship's booty was theirs and Ranaulf thought of his mother and father who were poor. He wanted nothing for himself, but felt their poverty in his heart. The bounty of wool, tin, and food would have been a treasure to the old couple. But how could he reach them?

All of a sudden, years of emotion came pouring into the boy's head and heart, and he wept. Captain Brendan led Ranaulf into his own cabin to talk. They spent hours together, talking and drinking into the cloudy, moonless night. The boy felt that a great weight had been lifted from his soul. Ranaulf explained everything that had happened – from the enchanted cup to the royal nursery, to his quest to find the cup again, to drink of it and regain his family. At last the man with the kind heart and unnatural eyes gave him a bear hug and put him to bed.

The next morning, Ranaulf felt better for having shared his secret with the captain. The captain felt a closeness with the boy for he was no stranger to the power of magic. Ranaulf ended up trading the dry goods from the pirate hoard for a suit of armor, which, he reasoned, would soon be useful to a knight-in-training such as himself.

Then there came an odd day when the fishing birds seemed to fly nearer to the ship, almost wanting to tell him something. The sunrise had been bright red, like a ruby necklace on the horizon. The clear sky and strong sun showed no portent of stormy weather to come. There was nothing much to do, so John and Ranaulf engaged in a game of chess as they often did. The *Cormorant* hugged the coast; *near,* thought the boy, *my old home in the forest.* He seemed to recognize the trees and the paths, the cliffs and the flowers from somewhere deep in his memory.

Captain Brendan stood outside searching for pirate ships through a crude telescope, but then the gulls began to dive at him. They seemed to be telling him something.

"Eeee, eeee," they screamed.

All of a sudden, Brendan threw down the telescope and dove into the sea like the bird after which his ship was named. His navy-blue coat sailed behind him. John and Ranaulf scrambled to the deck.

"No, no, Captain!" shouted John, a look of terror on his face.

Ranaulf leaned over the side of the *Cormorant* to see Brendan's lean body turn into that of a sea-monster as it submerged. First his arms, then his head, grew purple-green scales as he dove. When the captain's feet were no longer visible, a shining serpent swam in his place, lashing its huge dual-tipped tail to dive deeper and deeper into the sea.

Ranaulf moved away from the rail in horror. Was this the same mild and gentle man who had taken him under his wing? What was he doing? Ranaulf turned to John for help.

John knew the boy was afraid.

He said, "Do not fear, lad. You will see your friend again and he will not harm you. He has this ability to change himself into a sea creature, but it has a terrible effect on him and I fear for him. If only I knew what brought him to do this! My captain, my captain, come back safely," he cried softly.

Chapter Nine

The serpent, having spent some minutes below the surface, now rose up through the depths, pushing higher with his mighty tail, lashing the torrent of green until he appeared above the water with a tremendous splash and landed, as Brendan the man, on the deck of the *Cormorant*. He was soaked, shivering and weak with exhaustion. Then he crumbled into a sodden heap.

In his hands was the pewter cup.

Ranaulf stood as if made of stone. Was this man or beast? Brendan's eyes were calm, reflecting the cornflower blue of the heavens. The captain looked at Ranaulf and smiled weakly.

"Come to me, lad. Have you not been seeking this cup for years now?"

Slowly, step by step, Ranaulf walked toward the captain. The boy heard his friend's labored breathing. He brushed away the strands of dark hair that had stuck to Brendan's weary face. Brendan held the cup out to the boy and Ranaulf reached for it.

"Thank you, Captain. Now I may return to my family, but you must rest. Come, John and I will tend to you."

They carried their captain to his small quarters: a paneled room with a bed cut out of the wall. They made him comfortable and got him a cup of water to drink. Brendan rested his large hand upon that of Ranaulf.

"You are wondering, lad, if you touch man or beast. I am a bit of both, having crossed a lovely young mermaid who wanted me to become her husband. She had seen me at the helm and called me. Oh, son, she was a beautiful creature! Lithe, flowing like the water she lived in. It would have been so easy for me to leave my ship, to take on her life of wandering the sea without a care, but then I thought of good King Malcolm – how he trusted me to help with the security of his coasts. I had vowed my allegiance to him and I could not just disappear, so I told her *no* as gently as I could. She was angered and began to curse me. 'I will turn you into the sea itself and swim right through you as if you were nothing!' she hissed. I had to think fast.

"Already I felt my eyes watering, feeling strange and liquid, so I pulled a coin from my pocket, a square of copper that was most valuable thing I knew of. It was precious to me, being from the boat that Joseph of the Holy Land had used to transport the ancient metal of his mines in Cambren. Imprinted upon it were Roman words and numbers, which I could not read, but I recognized the image of Julius Caesar, making the tin very old, indeed.

"Maintaining eye contact with the creature, I lobbed the coin to her. She accepted it and turned it over in her soft, human hands, but then she became angry again and said to me:

'Land-dweller, you have tricked me out of my spell. But it has already begun and your eyes from this time on will be made of seawater. They will be the color of the sea; black, green, blue, even orange at the sunset and pink at the dawn. Men will fear you when you have such unnatural eyes and you will be forced to hide. But for your cleverness, I will give you the ability to turn yourself into a beast of the sea, to use when you see fit. This act will be costly to you. Each time you transform yourself, five years will be subtracted from your lifetime. Use it sparingly. Farewell.'

"With that she dove under and flicked her shining tail at me as if to wave goodbye. I didn't know what to think, but knew that my coin was gone, my eyes had changed, and I had acquired a strange power. I have used it only once before, to rescue a man overboard. But what are ten years of life? I have saved a man and have helped you to return home, son. I would make the choice again.

"So, today, when the gulls told me that the very cup you had quested for lay just below us, it was nothing to me to go after it. I just regret that such a fine lad as yourself will no longer be a hand on our ship. Do you recognize the land, Ranaulf?"

"Somehow, the cliff reminded me of something, but it was a formless feeling deep in my heart," Ranaulf replied. "I felt a longing as we approached this land, but could not define it. Now I know that it is called *home* and, somehow, things that seemed so important just months ago pale beside my need to see my parents again. I've been a terrible son. I knew, despite my youth, not to drink from that accursed cup, but I did it anyway and have been living a life of luxury, while my parents may be ill or starving. What could I have been thinking, trying to write in verse, when my parents know not their letters at all? They are near, I know it, and I will go to them and comfort them. I will at last be a good son."

Chapter Ten

As Ranaulf said those words, black clouds gathered along the coast. A storm was upon them. It had appeared without warning. Rain drenched them as the wind tossed the *Cormorant* up and down in rampant waves. The light gave way to darkness; the Narrow Sea became as dark as night.

A huge bolt of white lightning scarred the sky and Ranaulf looked helplessly at the captain in its eerie light. The next second, thunder shook the craft and the three friends reached for something onto which to hold. Ranaulf tasted saltwater in his mouth as it sprayed upon the deck.

"John, take the helm. Ranaulf, *listen to me*," the captain shouted over the noise of the storm. "The sea is angry with me. I have taken one of her treasures and she wants it back. **You must decide**. You may drink from the enchanted cup and save yourself. You may live out your days in happiness with your family. You can make real that feeling you know as 'home.' Or you can give up those dreams, lad, and return your treasure to the sea. For surely, if you do not, the *Cormorant* will lie as planks along the rocky coast."

The ship was rocking like a pendulum, helpless as a piece of driftwood upon the waves. Her sails were ripped from their masts as the *Cormorant* became a ragged skeleton, naked fore and aft.

How could he decide? All Ranaulf had wanted was to return to his grieving parents, to apologize for disobeying them and leaving them. He wanted to see them, if only for a moment, to show them that he was alive and in good health. He wanted to tell them that he loved them – and yet, he could not put his personal desires ahead of the lives of his shipmates. He could see that this supernatural storm would soon toss the *Cormorant* onto the rocks. The bark would split apart, sending his friends, Brendan and John, to a watery grave.

"Ranaulf!" screamed the captain, "You must choose **NOW**! What will you do?"

Ranaulf's heart broke as he forced his arm to throw the pewter cup back into the raging sea. That very second the wind calmed, the black clouds parted, and the waves became as white ripples on a glassy lake of blue. Ranaulf collapsed onto the deck and cried.

"Goodbye, mother; goodbye, father," he said through hot tears.

"I tried, lad," said Brendan, rubbing the boy's back. "I tried."

"I know, Captain."

"The sea will claim her own, Ranaulf. Perhaps you were meant for this life after all. You were very brave today. I will tell the king how you saved our lives. We are grateful."

Ranaulf returned to Caradon Hall. The events of that strange day had shaken him. He no longer dreamt of fair maidens nor adventures. Chivalry was a shallow act. He no longer hoped to see his parents, for even if he walked up to their cottage, the magic in the cup would prevent him from seeing them. Without the cup, he had no chance. Instead, he quietly performed his duties and remembered his humble roots. *I no longer aspire to greatness,* he thought solemnly. *I am still being punished for drinking of that dragon-molded cup.*

All in the castle noticed the change in his nature. Ranaulf became a serious lad. He fed, groomed, and exercised the horses with his head bowed low. He served at meals with his eyes averted. He solemnly attended to his lessons. He planned to live out his lonely life as a squire at Caradon Hall and resigned himself to never seeing his parents again.

Book Two

THE SNOW KING

Chapter One

For young Ranaulf, sleep usually came easily. As a squire in Caradon Hall, he was expected to serve meals, care for the horses, and learn chivalry and archery. But one winter night, Ranaulf could not sleep.

The hard, stone walls of the castle echoed with the cries of Queen Aurelia, who labored with her third child. Ranaulf hoped that the babe would be a boy, for the queen had borne two daughters, her beloved princesses, but no son. King Malcolm was ill and needed an heir to his throne. If the child were another girl, Malcolm's brother, Malachy, the cruel Duke of Malverne, would become the next king of Northborough.

Hedwidge, the midwife, attempted to comfort the queen. She used herbs and spells, but Queen Aurelia was in greater and greater pain. As she cried out, the boy felt helpless. Was his beautiful queen dying? She, who had so generously allowed him to stay in the castle to be raised with all he love and privilege of a true prince?

Outside, the night was cold and still. Stars sparkled in the black sky and the snowdrifts glistened in the moonlight. Ranaulf watched the fire dance in the torches adorning the walls.

He murmured a silent prayer, "Lord, protect my lady, the queen, from all harm this night."

At long last the child was born and his lusty cry was heard by the people in the castle.

They rejoiced as the midwife announced, "A boy! A son! An heir is born to the throne of Northborough."

The queen sighed in relief and happiness, the pain of childbirth all but forgotten in her joy.

"Let me see him, Hedwidge," she said.

But the old woman replied that she first needed to bathe and clothe the baby. She gave the queen a soothing tea to make her lady sleep.

Aurelia let her head fall upon the pillows. She felt as if she were weightless, the worry and physical burden of the child now lifted from her strong, but small, form. Golden hair surrounded her face like a halo. The queen smiled. She could not wait to comfort her newborn son in her arms.

"Hurry with the bath, Hedwidge, as my arms ache already for the feel of this child."

But as the midwife washed the blood from the child, some of it seemed to stick. She scrubbed harder and harder, causing the babe to wail, but the blood would not wash off. The boy had a stain the color of port-wine on his left cheek. It was an ominous sign, most especially as the midwife was a superstitious woman.

Hedwidge wrapped the baby securely in white wool and took him from the birthing room to find Medard, the sorcerer.

The queen's mind was becoming foggy, yet she cried out, "My baby! I...want to...hold...my...son."

Then the sleeping potion took its full effect and Aurelia closed her eyes.

Hedwidge ran with the child to the sorcerer's chamber. *Medard will know what to do,* she thought. She hurried up the curling stone staircase with her bundle tight in her arms. She hoped not to be seen, so as not to be questioned.

30

The wizard lived high up in a turret with one small, rectangular arrow slit. He was a powerful man in the kingdom as his advice was sought in all matters of life and death.

He was also a close friend of the Duke of Malverne.

Chapter Two

Medard wore richly-dyed indigo-blue robes and golden rings. His white, cloud-like hair grew not just from the top of his head, but from most of his face as well. He fixed his pale, empty eyes upon Hedwidge as she entered his chamber and showed him the boy. She felt as if he had been expecting her.

He looked at the baby's face in the yellow light of a dozen costly beeswax candles. Then he backed away from the child, pretending to look horrified at the blood-like mark.

In secret, Medard could not believe his good luck in finding so easy a way to end the dynasty of the benevolent ruling family. The wheels of his evil mind began to turn.

"This child is *cursed* and he will cause the curse to fall upon the entire kingdom! There will be bloodshed as long as he lives and far worse if he ever became king. The wine-stain on his cheek portends the spilling of our blood by our enemies. They will attack and be victorious!" foretold the sorcerer.

He thought for a few minutes and formed a wicked plan.

Just then, Squire Ranaulf walked by to see what was happening. He had followed Hedwidge at a distance.

"Lad, your name," demanded Medard.

"Ranaulf, milord."

"Can you prepare a mount immediately? The safety of the kingdom depends on it."

The lad ran out to the stables and saddled his knight's horse, which was swifter than his own old mare. He ascended the dark, narrow staircase to tell Medard that he was ready.

"Ranaulf, come here," the wizard ordered the frightened young man. "Take this accursed infant deep into the woods. He is under a spell of bad blood. You can see it for yourself. To break the spell, you must dig a grave of snow and place him in it, then cover him over and lay a branch of hemlock atop the mound. Stay there until you no longer hear his cries. Report to me afterwards."

Ranaulf was so surprised that he stood motionless, staring at the sorcerer.

"Did you not understand my instructions, Squire? You are in a position to save our whole kingdom!"

He slapped the speechless young man hard against the face.

"So, hurry now! Be off," commanded Medard.

Ranaulf had no choice but to obey.

Chapter Three

He took the baby, barely seven pounds, into his arms and descended the cold, gray stairs to the stables where his master's good horse was waiting for him. He rode over the drawbridge and out of the castle into the frigid winter night. No one saw him leave. He cradled the child in his left arm and held the reins in his right hand.

Once he was out in the open, he spurred the horse along and looked over his shoulder. He was not being followed. Before long, the first rays of sun reached over the horizon and it was morning.

Ranaulf came to a place in the woods where he could build the mound. He first laid a blanket down in the snow and placed the baby upon it. The infant had fallen asleep from the rhythmic trot of the horse. *I must not look at him,* thought the lad, for Ranaulf was afraid that he would feel sympathy for the doomed infant if he but saw his face. Of course, his glance fell upon that of the child after all – and his heart melted. The tiny face was beautiful and peaceful. The red mark did not worry the young man in the least. He did not believe in curses.

Ranaulf knew that he could never leave the young prince in the snow to die. He suspected that Malachy and the wizard had planned this murder as a path to their own power. However, he knew that to disobey would mean his own death.

The lad had a plan. He worked fast and dug a burial mound, then he quietly walked through the woods with his bow and quiver of arrows. Before long, he killed a rabbit. He cut down a hemlock bough with his dagger and brought these two things back to the grave.

The baby had not slept long because of the cold. He began to stir and look for his mother. Ranaulf gently removed his woolen garments and wrapped the child in a saddle blanket. He dripped some of the hare's blood onto the infant's clothes and tore them. He also dripped the blood onto the snowy grave. Then he pushed the rabbit's carcass into the snow and made it look as if there had been a struggle. He placed the carcass into his leather hunting pouch, tied the bloodied swaddling clothes to his saddle, and laid the hemlock branch over the grave.

Chapter Four

Once again, Ranaulf mounted his knight's horse. He carried the little prince in his arms. The horse galloped deeper into the tangled woods. The lad knew that the child must be hungry, so he made his way through the forest as fast as possible.

Soon he came upon the small wattle-and-daub cottage belonging to Master Julian and Mistress Anne. Julian greeted Ranaulf as he tied his horse to a tree. Julian was a trapper and he sold skins and furs to the merchants in the castle. He was a simple man, with a thick beard and coarse clothes. Then his wife, Anne, came to the door.

"Please, come inside, young man."

She noticed the little bundle that he carried. Anne took the baby from Ranaulf and held him close to her heart.

"Whose child is this? Surely not your own?"

"He is the newborn prince of Northborough."

The old couple was surprised to hear the story of the child's birth, but they understood why Ranaulf had brought him to their humble cottage. It was his sole chance to remain alive.

"You have done a brave and wise deed," said Julian. "Come and have a cup of mead to warm yourself."

As they drank at the oaken table, Anne sat near the fire, cradling the boy in her arms and kissing his cheek. The prince became warm and rosy.

"Will you raise the babe here in secrecy?" Ranaulf asked.

Already, Anne wept soft tears of joy. The couple did not have any children of their own and she was filled with happiness to be a mother at last. She loved the little boy who had now become her son.

"I shall call him 'Rory' for his red cheek and hair," she said and kissed him again.

But Ranaulf was still concerned about the little one's safety. He had seen the fire in the sorcerer's eyes. He warned Julian.

"No one from the court must ever see him, for he would be recognized by the mark on his face. He must live alone in the forest and you must teach him to be quiet, and to survive alone if ever he must flee. Should the Duke's soldiers ever see him, both you and the boy would be killed."

"I understand," said Julian. "Thank you for trusting us."

"Yes, thank you," Anne added. "I will begin to sew his clothes tonight. You need not worry about him, my friend."

Ranaulf went to his horse, gave Julian the rabbit for its coat and for stew, and said goodbye. Then he rushed back to the castle.

Chapter Five

A groom met him at the stable.

"You are wanted by the sorcerer at once," he said and took the horse.

Ranaulf went upstairs to meet Medard.

He reminded himself to be confident. Ranaulf straightened his back and ascended the stairs to the musty turret room, but before he entered, he heard the white-haired man upbraid a boy, just younger than himself, for bungling the mixing of a potion. Ranaulf peered around the stone wall through a crack in the door to witness the trembling lad, wringing his thick fingers in fear, his pudgy, blank face turned down to avoid meeting the penetrating gaze of Medard.

"It was the simplest task that I could give you! One thimbleful of the snake's venom added to the simmering cauldron at the fire. Any simpleton could have executed it without thinking, but you – *YOU* – my own apprentice, spills it. Do you know how hard it is to gather even a thimbleful of snake's venom? Well, you shall find out! Go now, collect it yourself, and do not come back into my presence without it!"

Ranaulf felt terrible for the boy, but knew that he had an audience with the sorcerer and could not be any later than he was. It would put the young prince's life in further danger. He resolved to help the boy with the gathering of venom later in the day.

The frightened child stumbled past him, having been thrown out of the room by the sorcerer. Ranaulf detained him by holding onto the poor child's shoulder. He spoke to the apprentice in low tones.

"Don't worry, my friend. I will assist you later. I am armed and will be able to spear some of your quarry with my sword," Ranaulf whispered as he helped the boy to his feet. "Now, off you go. Be of good cheer."

The squire mentally prepared himself for the meeting and entered.

"Milord," he said and bowed low.

"Have you completed your mission?" asked the evil man, who already could taste power in his mouth.

"I have."

"You have been gone longer than we had expected. It is noon already–" said the wizard, leaving off his sentence and allowing a pause to sit heavily between them.

"Milord, I dug the grave of snow as you asked, but the miserable child was crying so loudly that a wolf heard him. Before I could cover him with snow, the wolf attacked and took the boy. I lingered to make sure he lived no longer and bring you these garments as proof."

Ranaulf handed the bloody clothes to Medard.

"You have done well, squire. Speak of this to no one. The queen has been told that her son died of hemorrhage an hour after his birth."

Then Medard pressed a large gold coin into Ranaulf's hand.

"You are dismissed."

"Thank you, milord."

Ranaulf bowed and went back to his small room, trembling inside. He could only hope that the little prince would survive and never be discovered. Then he pushed the gold coin down a mouse hole and went outside to find the apprentice.

Chapter Six

He was not hard to find. His was the lonely figure, tall as a deer, walking the land beyond the castle walls with his head down, looking, as Ranaulf knew, for serpents. Ranaulf chuckled mildly to himself, since he could imagine the boy running full speed in the *other* direction should he ever encounter his prey. The lad wore a gray woollen cloak, closed at his neck with a pewter clasp in the shape of an oak leaf, but it was not enough against the chill. He felt sorry for the boy, for his humiliation, and for his cold.

Ranaulf strode up to him and asked his name.

"I am called Giles, sir, when my master is not calling me *slow-witted* or *cloven-handed*. I was given to him because of a proficiency in *knowing* things, sir, such things as not known to others, but all of this memorizing of spells and mixing of draughts has my mind all flustered. It is too much for me as I have only just learned my letters, even."

Ranaulf looked into the eyes of Giles, amazed at their amber color. He had never seen such eyes before. The boy had a sweet countenance and soft, wispy brown hair that framed his face in a flattering way under his winter cap. This had been knit of gray wool and it tightly hugged the boy's head.

"First of all, Giles, you must stop calling me *sir*. I am merely a squire, just older than yourself and nearly as new at everything. Call me by my Christian name, Ranaulf, and treat me as a brother."

He unsheathed his sword and held it ready should they come upon a snake as they walked.

"Snakes, be warned!" he shouted.

Giles laughed.

Then Ranaulf said softly, "Tell me about your master, Medard."

The boy looked into the squire's blue eyes.

"I will tell you of my first acquaintance with him, just a full moon ago when I received my initial lesson. We were alone, as always, in that dark chamber of his. He lit a single candle and held it to my face. It seemed that he was evaluating me, but he looked so deeply into my eyes that I feared he would see into my mind itself. I wanted my mother and I began to tremble. I reminded myself to be strong and asked the master if there was anything I could do for him.

"'You will not speak unless spoken to! Is that understood?' he roared at me and I answered that I did understand. 'Now read to me the first page of the book on the ledge.' I walked over to the shriveled, dust-covered tome beneath the window. The pages themselves were dark from years of the smoke of tapers. I had a sense of foreboding, but opened the book nevertheless. As I opened the cover, a hundred little insects crawled out in all directions. I screamed and slammed down the cover, causing a cloud of dust to rise above it. I turned to face the master.

"'Giles, you must not be afraid of our little friends, the crawling ones. They that crawl can aid us in many ways. You think that because of the gift of your forward-seeing eyes that you can escape the more mundane instruction in the dark arts? No, child, put away your pride. You will learn, from page one, all that has been transmitted to me. My hair has turned white and I can see that my days here are near their end, yet there is much to do. I will have you learn the secrets of the crawling ones, intimately, by living one night with them.'

"He grabbed me and shoved me into the armoire. I heard the key turning in the lock. It was totally dark. I could feel insects crawling around me: spiders, ants, centipedes, who knows? I could not see them, but I was forced to feel them and the armoire was so small that I couldn't move. I couldn't scratch; I couldn't even lie down for the night. That didn't matter because I couldn't sleep anyway. It was horrifying. But Medard got his way and I never ran from insects any more. He taught me a lesson, not to fear them, but I learned something else – that he was a cruel old man."

"Listen, Giles," said Ranaulf, "I will make a pact with you. I will help you whenever I can and will you allow me, in return, to call upon your skills, someday, should I be in need of assistance?"

"Meager as they are, sir, they will be at your disposal."

"Giles, my friend, please do not call me *sir*."

"Ranaulf, from now on I shall call you my friend."

And they walked along, heads down, looking for snakes.

Chapter Seven

The kingdom deeply mourned the loss of the little prince. Queen Aurelia was overcome with grief and stayed in her chamber day and night. The poor king, already old and sickly, did not survive the tragedy. He died within a week of the birth and the supposed death of his son and sole heir.

Now the royal family consisted of the queen and her two daughters, who were not permitted to rule. Thus the Duke of Malverne became King of Northborough in a magnificent coronation ceremony. No expense was spared. There was mead, dancing, and food for all. King Malachy's banner, *Sable a Dragon rampant Or,* hung from the outside castle walls. Medard became his Lord Chancellor and was more powerful than ever.

One of the king's first acts was to increase taxes on the peasants. They were to pay a greater portion of their harvest to the king. The people suffered when there was a poor harvest that fall, for they had very little with which to feed their families.

Meanwhile, the opulence of the court became known throughout the countryside. Meals were served on golden dishes and wine was drunk from silver cups. The king ordered tapestries of unicorns to adorn the walls, but once again, he was in need of money, so the Lord Chancellor suggested taxing the tradesmen. Carpenters, blacksmiths, jewelers, and other guild members were forced to pay a large portion of their earnings to the king, but King Malachy continued his lavish lifestyle, importing rare and expensive silk, spices, and amber from far-away lands. The Lord Chancellor saw that the merchants were making a great fortune from this trade, so he suggested that the kingdom tax all trading. The merchants were furious. These wealthy men began to grumble against the king.

Chapter Eight

In the forest, Rory had grown tall, strong, and wise. He loved his adoptive parents and knew nothing of his royal lineage. Julian had taught him his own profession of trapping and how to survive in the woods. Rory could hunt, fish, build a fire, and defend himself against any enemy – man or animal.

At times he encountered other young men trapping or hunting in the deep woods. They complained about the new taxes that were burdening their families. Rory decided to talk to his father about the government.

"Can nothing be done?" he asked. "King Malachy squanders our money, while we are forced to sell land to pay taxes. If there were an uprising, I would become part of it."

"Why do you not organize an armed force yourself, son? You know many who would join you. Many who, like you, are accurate with a bow and arrow."

"Why not, indeed," said Rory, "I believe that I shall."

Julian knew it was time to tell his son who he really was. The boy was fast turning into a man and a sturdy and honest one at that. His face was fair, with scattered freckles concentrating upon his nose and cheeks. The port-wine stain was almost a mark of dignity. His wavy, orange-red hair covered his strong and massive shoulders. His bones were big; his legs were like tree trunks. The young man's green eyes had a yellow ring around the center, almost like the golden circlet his mother, the queen, had worn – but the lad wore the simple clothes and shoes of a peasant, never knowing his true lineage. *Now was the right time to tell him,* thought Julian.

He told Rory of the malevolent plot to kill him and of the kind page who had saved his life. Rory listened in amazement. Slowly he touched the reddish mark on his left cheek.

Am I under a curse? he wondered.

He blamed himself for his natural father's death and for the misfortune that had befallen the kingdom. But Julian could tell what Rory was thinking.

"No, no, it is not your fault, son. Royal blood flows through your veins and you were born to rule Northborough. Do not become melancholy. Even if you ruled after your father's death, you would have been forced to battle King Malachy and the Lord Chancellor. They have always craved the throne for themselves. They would have fought you from within the castle walls, which may have been harder. Now, at least, you can see your enemy and fight him in the open."

"Thank you, father," said Rory with thoughtfulness.

So, together, the father and the son began to construct weapons. They made bows, arrows, swords, and knives. Rory recruited a small band of rebels and they met in secret to plot strategy. After a time, they were ready.

Chapter Nine

Rory's men rode out of the forest at dawn. The dew still clung to the grass. It would be a sunny, warm day – a good day for battle.

The soldiers wore no armor or mail. They were simple people who could not afford such luxuries, but their hearts burned with love for their kingdom. If necessary, they were willing to give their lives for the cause.

The men waited for the drawbridge to be lowered for a merchant leaving the castle. Then they overcame the guards and entered Caradon Hall.

Rory raised his sword and announced, "People of Northborough, in the name of justice, I have come to depose King Malachy."

The king's soldiers surrounded the rebels. They were badly outnumbered. But then one of the king's men saw the red stain on Rory's cheek. It was Ranaulf.

Ranaulf explained to the other knights who was the intruder. When they heard his story, the royal knights refused to fight and came over to Rory's side. Just then, Medard, the Lord Chancellor, now a bitter and elderly man, left his room to see what was happening downstairs.

He was sickened to see his soldiers banded around the outlaw, Rory, but as he came closer, he recognized the young man's face. It was the face of the infant whom he had ordered put to death many winters ago. But here the prince was alive and well, commanding a small army.

Before Medard could give any orders, he was surrounded by the tips of drawn swords. He was bound and led to a prison cell in the tower. As King Malachy descended the stairs, he, too, was captured and sent to the tower, cursing and screaming the whole way there. The people of the castle were overjoyed. They hailed Rory as their new king.

"All hail the king! Long live the king!" they shouted.

It did not seem to bother anyone that he had a port-wine stain on his cheek.

"Please lead me to Queen Aurelia," requested the conqueror.

A few of the royal knights walked him to her chamber. As he entered her room, the queen saw a young man who looked very much like her late husband, Malcolm. There was the same square face, the large features capable of expressing the deepest of human emotions, the cascade of fiery vermilion-red curls resting upon the shoulder. The solid build, powerful as the river which turned the grain mill. And the eyes, green as the hills surrounding their home, with a circle of yellow inside of them like the corona of the sun and framed with nearly-white feathered lashes. The only seeming difference was the purple-red stain upon her son's left cheek. But, in her opinion, the stain only added to his masculine appeal.

Yes, this lad had to be her son, the image of his father, the late king. The sight of him took Aurelia's breath away, but she remembered to keep her composure.

She straightened her back, held her head high, and asked him, "Are you my son, whom I have believed dead all these years?"

"I am, milady," answered Rory, bowing and kissing her hand.

"Then let me hold you," Queen Aurelia said and wept as she embraced him.

Then she wanted to know how it was that he was alive.

"Midwife Hedwidge told me that you had died, dear one."

Rory told his mother the story of the young page who had saved him and all about his adoptive parents at the cottage. The queen sent for Ranaulf.

"I am at your service, milady," he said upon arriving. Queen Aurelia remembered the brave, young squire.

Chapter Ten

"Was it you who saved my son?"

"It was my honor to do so, milady," Squire Ranaulf replied.

"Then you are to receive the highest honor of Northborough for rescuing my son. You have my deepest and everlasting gratitude for your brave and kind deed. You shall be knighted and made a member of the Order of the White Hare, an ancient fellowship that has met at Caradon Hall since the Romans left and my husband's forebears established a government here. In addition, whenever you wish, you may ask of me any boon and I will grant it," said Queen Aurelia.

"Thank you, milady, though I deserve nothing for doing naught but my duty to the king," said Ranaulf as he bowed low.

Then one of the soldiers came into the queen's chambers with a cloth in his hand.

"We found this in the Lord Chancellor's room, hidden in a false book," he said.

Rory did not know what it was, but Ranaulf did.

"Milord, those were the very clothes you wore when I carried you into the woods the first day of your life. I dipped the blood of a rabbit onto them, to prove to Medard that you were dead," explained the squire.

Rory examined the tiny garments.

"Then these are for you, milady," he said to the aged queen whose eyes had filled with tears, "for they were sewn by your own hands for your own son."

He gently kissed her cheek and she kissed the little clothes, pressing them to her heart. Then Rory thought of the sorcerer Medard.

"He would have me buried alive in a snowy grave," he said and became sad.

But Ranaulf changed the subject.

"Milord, here we have the basis for a new coat of arms: the white snow and the red blood. Let Malachy's banners be removed from the castle walls and your own be unfurled instead."

He did not want Rory to fall into melancholy and so it was done. The *Sable a Dragon rampant Or* came down and the *Argent goutty de sang* flew proudly over Caradon Hall.

It was the beginning of a long and prosperous reign for King Rory, the Snow King. His coronation was lovely, but simple. Food and drink were given freely to peasants, merchants, and members of the court alike.

King Rory often rode to the secluded cottage in the forest where he had grown up. He brought food for Julian and Anne; they would take nothing more. He loved them dearly and remained their devoted and grateful son.

The deposed king and the Lord Chancellor spent the rest of their lives in the stone cells of the tower. They remained angry and hateful to the end.

For a long time, Northborough lived at peace with its neighbors. There had never been a curse upon the little boy that was born to Queen Aurelia on that cold, white night.

Chapter Eleven

The queen mother did not forget her promises to Ranaulf. One day, still fringed with the crisp frost of March, she called him to her chamber.

"Brave Ranaulf, the time has come to prepare yourself for the ceremony of knighthood. Tonight, you are to appear before Sir Prosper and Sir Leofric in the great hall. They will be your sponsors. Once again, thank you for saving the life of my son."

Ranaulf noticed a tear well up in his queen's eye. She would not allow it to fall, though, until she had hidden her face by embracing him.

"Go, thou, in peace," she said with true gratitude in her voice.

That evening Ranaulf waited in the great hall. He was extremely nervous, to say the least. He had heard stories about the knighting ceremony, but details were kept secret and he did not know what to expect. He tapped his foot and hummed little songs to himself, trying to stay calm.

His two sponsors entered the hall and conducted Ranaulf to the bath – a tub carved out of stone. Water was heated in the fireplace, carried in and poured into the tub. Tonight, because of the ceremony, rose petals of the deepest red floated upon the water, releasing their sweet perfume. Seated upon the tub's edge was an older knight, Sir Prosper.

He held a sharp blade, with which he shaved the hair from Ranaulf's head. Prosper was a kind and warm-hearted man who did not like fighting and killing. Instead, he ran errands for the king, which took a great deal of time. But Prosper was more than happy to convey messages from one kingdom to another upon his best friend, his horse, which enjoyed the journey as much as its rider.

Prosper often sang while traveling; his voice was not bad at all. His cheekbones were wide and he trimmed his brown mustache and beard so perfectly that not one hair ever appeared out of place. His brown eyes were kind, with crow's feet forming at the corners. But most people remembered Prosper for his eyebrows, which nearly always tilted up at the center, giving him a perpetual look of surprise and interest in whatever his companion of the moment was saying.

Linen hangings surrounded the bath, giving it privacy. Sir Leofric sat upon the edge of the tub next to Sir Prosper and began a long lecture. Leofric was a man who resembled the lion for whom he was named. He combed his long, wavy hair straight back from his rugged face, whereupon it rose a little, giving him a ferocious mien. He lost his temper easily, but apologized with equal speed. He was fearless; strong, yet always willing to perform the most unpleasant tasks. He talked to Ranaulf about chivalry, honor, honesty, respect, and dignity. He felt silly lecturing this squire about bravery, but it was part of the formula. Leofric spelled out the duties of those inducted into the Order of the White Hare, about meetings, and the responsibilities of the king's guard.

"It is like becoming his brother," he said, looking steadily into Ranaulf's eyes.

Ranaulf promised to obey in all things and took an oath of secrecy. His sponsors poured vases of bathwater over the young man's head, making the sign of the cross over him. It was as if Ranaulf were baptized again, this time into manhood.

He left the warmth of the bath, dried off, and was dressed by his sponsors in the coarse, brown wool of a hermit's tunic. Prosper and Leofric walked him into the chapel of Caradon Hall. This little room, although lacking a window, glowed with the soft and inviting light of many cream-colored beeswax candles. The stone altar was covered in an intricate lace cloth. Upon the altar stood the candles and a crucifix. Below it lay the bones of saints and below the floor rested the bones of the previous kings and queens of Northborough.

Ranaulf's armor was placed before him. He was told that he must stand throughout the night, making an exhaustive examination of conscience, meditating and praying for the strength and grace from God to become a good knight. With that, the sponsors left Ranaulf to his thoughts.

They returned at dawn to bathe the candidate once again. The young man, dressed in his hermit's tunic, confessed to the priest and heard Mass. It was the custom then to offer a burning taper with a coin stuck as near to the flame as possible to the priest.

Ranaulf was led to his room to sleep. He had fulfilled his role well, wanting to sit, to kneel down, during the long and silent night, but remaining steadfast and upon his two feet. Now he felt clean, light, like the wind; as though his cares had all been washed away. He felt as though he could just lift off the ground and soar above it; soar to the land beyond the Narrow Sea or even further. He felt close to his parents again and when he slept, his mother came to him in a dream and kissed his forehead.

Chapter Twelve

Ranaulf awoke to Prosper and Leofric sitting at the foot of his bed. The day was breezy and cool. Bulbs seemed unsure as to whether or not to let their green stems reach above the ground.

His sponsors dressed Ranaulf in fine clothes and led him to the great hall. King Rory awaited him, knelt before his young rescuer, and placed a golden spur upon the candidate's right shoe. Sir Prosper knelt and fastened the left one. Sir Leofric held out a sword – and what a sword! The blade, thick and heavy, had been recently sharpened and polished, yet here and there were blemishes that could not be removed.

This sword has seen battle before, thought Ranaulf as he gazed upon it. He was fascinated by the workmanship of the hilt, which was in the shape of a cross. Embedded within the cross lay two lines of precious stones. From the top to the bottom, they began with a clear crystal and turned to jasper yellow, golden topaz, rose quartz, and at last a ruby scarlet. These were the colors of the sun. From one side to the other, the colors ranged from aquamarine blue to deep forest green. These were the colors of the sea. Ranaulf began to get an idea of where he had seen these colors before.

"A gift," said Leofric, "to you from Captain Brendan of the *Cormorant*. I know not how he had knowledge of this ceremony, nor how his messenger appeared here just this morning after riding from the coast, but the captain sends you his congratulations and best wishes."

Ranaulf opened a small parchment scroll. Brendan had written:

I was not always a sailor, lad. Once I had been a soldier and I give to you my sword Mermaid's Curse. *Be thou a good knight.*

Ranaulf had to hold back tears. The memories of John, Brendan, and himself living together upon the ship; of John's good company and the captain's dive below the water, becoming a sea monster to pluck his mother's pewter cup from the floor of the sea and becoming a man again, drained of five years of his life for him, a mere boy. Then his awful face, his eyes now black as the raging storm, yelling at him, "You must choose **NOW**! What will you do?" and Ranaulf tossing the cup back, appeasing the angry sea, saving their lives and forsaking his chance of ever returning home.

"Augh," he said, physically suffering as he relived those moments in his mind. But Brendan had not forgotten him and must be somehow watching over him, with his magical eyes, his irises reflecting without fail the color of the sea.

The hilt of his new sword was encrusted with jewels the color of Brendan's eyes. Ranaulf did not know how the captain had come to possess such a sword even before the mermaid's curse, but he accepted that there were things in this world beyond the understanding of humans. This sword was one such thing.

"Are you all right?" Leofric asked.

Ranaulf looked up from his reverie and nodded.

"Do you accept the sword *Mermaid's Curse*?"

"I do."

Sir Leofric girded the sword upon the young man's belt. Although no one present knew it, at that moment, far away at sea, the captain was scanning the horizon for pirate ships. His eyes mirrored the blue-green teal of the water and they remained that color for the rest of the man's foreshortened life.

Leofric kissed Ranaulf on the cheek, saying, "Be thou a good knight. Follow the commandments of God. Obey thy liege lord, the king."

Ranaulf drew his sword and offered it to the priest, who returned it to him. The ceremonial part was over. The young man was exhausted. He felt light-headed and dizzy. Too many memories had crowded into his head.

Ranaulf, now a knight of the Order of the White Hare of Northborough, quietly slipped away from the feast that followed. He needed time to think. He retreated to his room where he sat upon the bed, staring at the sword and contemplating his mother, his father, and the pewter cup.

Book Three

THREE SISTERS

Chapter One

Three sisters had spent the day outdoors, picking flowers in the mild sunshine.

"Cigfa, your thistles are so showy. They make a pretty bouquet. But do their thorns not cut your fingers?"

"I am not concerned with small cuts as they enhance my appearance. But, for now, I use a salve that keeps my hands soft as a lambskin."

"Perhaps you will share it with me," said Branwen, "as these rosemary and pine cuttings are quite sharp."

"I shall, of course. But, Rhiannon, why so quiet? Did you find those delicate forget-me-nots by the brook that you searched for? They're lovely, you know."

"I did, sister, but now I am bored. I am tired of picking flowers. Aren't you?"

"Yes, but I think I've just found something even more fun to do. Look ahead to the edge of the meadow. There rides a young man, strong of shoulder and comely of face. And his beard! It is red as the robin's breast. I should like to have him," Branwen said, her emerald green eyes shining.

"Is he one of us?" wondered Cigfa, who noticed the port-wine stain on the young man's cheek.

Sometimes, the fates marked people to whom they had given special powers.

"No, sister," replied Rhiannon, "he is human and of royal blood, I can sense it."

"Let us see which one of us wins his heart," Cigfa said, freeing her long lilac-colored hair from its braid.

It would be a welcome diversion. She rubbed the salve on her fingers, making them soft as a babe's.

Rory rode with caution across the meadow. He knew that, without the cover of the forest, there was danger. The small birds he had caught hung on either side of his saddle, tied with leather jesses. It had been a long day, hunting with his hawk, but a profitable one. He patted his horse's rump.

"Good girl, Cymbeline."

She was white throughout, but for her soft brown eyes. Her legs were not long. She was gentle and a good companion for her master. Her ears picked up; she had sensed something.

When the king looked up, there, in the middle of the meadow, was a table and two chairs. In the center of the table was a tall, crudely glazed vase of thistles. The table was loaded with delicacies of all kinds: light pastry, thick custard, and milk whipped into stiffness. There were glazed cups filled with a honey-like nectar. And there was a young woman sitting in one of the chairs, looking hopefully at him with amethyst eyes.

She blinked. Her eyelashes were the color of twilight on a mountain. She wore a flowing violet-colored gown and sprigs of lavender graced her hair. Rory had never seen so extraordinary a woman. She was a vision of supernatural loveliness.

"Come and sit with me," Cigfa said. "You've been hunting all day. Surely you would like a sip of nectar, a bite of cake?"

Rory felt confused. He *was* hungry and longed to sit next to this beautiful young woman, so like a butterfly. But her sudden appearance in the meadow, where there had been nothing but prairie grasses, and her knowledge of his activities during the day warned him to be cautious. Things were happening too fast.

"Lady," he said, "your hospitality overwhelms me, but I am a simple man of simple tastes. I dine from a trencher of old bread filled with tough beef and fear that such delicacies as you offer would upset my humors. Perhaps another time, my Lilac Lady."

At that, Cigfa became enraged.

"How dare you reject my hospitality?! I have set this banquet for you and you will not even sit at table with me? A curse on you! I will put enmity between you and your first-born son!"

As Rory stared, the mauve woman transformed before his eyes into a horrible witch. First, she chanted in an ancient tongue that he could not understand, but he knew her meaning as she pointed at him and stared, while uttering the words of the curse. Then she flew off into the sky and toward a castle ahead, which appeared to be made of the very sweets of which the table had been set. Cigfa circled the keep three times, with a hideous laugh, before entering through a window. The table disappeared, leaving Rory breathless, his heart pounding. After a few minutes, he regained composure.

"That was close," he said to himself. "I must be more careful. I almost supped with that witch at her enchanted table and she may have made me prisoner of her castle."

Cymbeline neighed nervously as if to give her consent and the king mounted with some unsteadiness. But Rory's bright mood, gained from a good day hawking, eventually returned. He clicked to his horse and took up the reins.

Chapter Two

King Rory had become the ruler of Northborough, although by his humble mien and clothing, people who did not know him did not recognize him as their leader. Rory liked this idea as it enabled him to ride through the land, seeing how the villagers, the tenants, and the merchants were doing. He questioned them about their crops, their animals, and their trade. He inquired about their health. In this way, he received truthful information from the honest men and women of his kingdom.

Rory came to feel that the people wanted to have as much freedom as possible to earn a living and to raise their children, while knowing that the king, his knights, and soldiers were there to protect them from enemies. Rory was happy to run his fief in that manner, which worked well in normal times. He deliberately kept the taxes low and rescinded the onerous burdens that had beenn imposed by his predecessor, his uncle, King Malachy. From these casual visits to his people, Rory learned that the office of Lord Chancellor was not needed; as lord of the land, he was perfectly capable of making decrees and seeing they were enforced.

The common peasants knew little of the fine workings of Rory's government, but they did know that their families were more prosperous, their children fatter, and that they could stow away a little coinage or preserves or salted meat for a rainy day. They loved their liege as they had loved Good King Malcolm, the young king's father.

Since the kingdom was at peace with its neighbors, it meant that fathers and sons stayed home to tend the fields and livestock, rather than venture to foreign soil, probably to return wounded if not at all. This period of peace resulted from the fine knights dedicated to King Rory and their joy in serving their lord with fidelity and tirelessness. They were well-armed and owned fine horses. No bordering kingdom desired to attack Northborough, so peace spread like clover in the grass.

Peace and prosperity, the two pillars of Rory's governance, made him a beloved leader of the people. This love of his people, in turn, made Rory a happier and more good-humored man that he had been before as nothing pleased him more than to be viewed as a benevolent ruler.

Chapter Three

Rory rode on at an easy pace. He inhaled deeply of the sweet meadow scent. He was on his way back; he could see the path through the forest that would bring him home. Together, Cymbeline and Rory made a long shadow across the tall grass. His horse was a worthy specimen for a king; pure white mane and tail compact, strong and not overly large. One of the things Rory liked best about Cymbeline was her good judgment. She often seemed wiser than humans.

Horse and rider stopped short at the edge of the woods. There, a young woman, Branwen, reclined on a woolen blanket. She was wrapped in a gown that seemed to be made from the wings of a Luna moth. Her long, olive-green hair was braided through with strands of ivy. She was staring into a transparent ball, clear as water, but cloudy inside. The white clouds moved around like dandelion seeds on the wind.

Astounding, thought Rory.

"Come and sit with me," Branwen said, gesturing with a graceful hand. "You've been hunting all day. Surely you would like to see the future in my telling-ball. Or, if you like, let me reveal your fortune from these cards."

Rory looked down at the beautiful, feminine creature, so like a wood-sprite, holding richly illuminated cards in her hand, which pictured members of a royal family, the Devil, and others. They were decorated as intricately as the pages of the holy books copied by monks. They even seemed to gleam in places where pure gold paint had been used for highlights. Rory had never seen such cards before. Who would not like to know the future?

He considered Branwen's offer. As monarch, such knowledge could be helpful. *What will the harvest be like this year? Will enemies attack our realm? Do the people need a new mill or shall I have the walls of the castle reinforced?* But, remembering the table of delicacies and the Lilac Lady, Rory decided that he had best decline. Besides, Cymbeline's ears were standing upright again. She exhaled sharply, almost as a sign of disgust.

The mare tossed her head back as if to say, "Woman, you are not worth our time."

"Lady," the king said, "your kind offer overwhelms me, but I am a simple man of simple faith. All my life I have trusted in God and I must continue to do so, knowing that He will provide for my needs. Yes, it would be a wondrous thing to peer into the hidden days to come, but then a different burden would rest upon my shoulders – to make the proper decisions, knowing what my advisors and the court would not know. I cannot pretend to be more than human and it is all I aspire to be. I am afraid that I am resigned to making my share of mistakes like everyone else. But, thank you, *mademoiselle*, nevertheless."

Branwen became enraged.

"How dare you reject my offer? I could unwrap your future like a parchment map of the countryside, give you more power than princes, and you will not even sit here with me on the meadow? A curse on you! When your days come to an end, you will be slain by a member of your own family."

Rory watched, transfixed, as this mossy-green vixen stared at him, pointing and uttering the old and nearly-forgotten language of witches. He knew that he had been cursed and a shudder of ice went through his veins. Branwen flew off into the sky, toward another castle just ahead, which appeared to be made of branches and boughs of evergreen trees rather than of stone. The witch circled the keep three times, laughing ominously, before entering through a window. The blanket she had sat on rose up and flew after her, leaving Rory wide-eyed in astonishment.

"I must be more careful," the king spoke to himself.

He shook in the saddle, frightened by the two evil women. He entered the woods, telling himself that he did not believe in curses. It was cool and twilight. He wanted to get home. The witches were right; he was hungry and tired. But upon hearing the rushing of a brook, he tied Cymbeline to a tree and dismounted. His horse happily munched the moist, supple grass.

Chapter Four

Rory walked down to the cold stream, gulping cupfuls of the refreshing water and splashing his sweaty face.

"Ahhhhh," he said, feeling much better.

But then he noticed a water-nymph in the stream, with one wing caught in the mouth of a very large rainbow trout. She was struggling for her life, kicking and flapping her free wing. Rory threaded his arrow into his bow and with great skill pierced the fish, which he lifted from the water. He freed the nymph, then held her in the palm of his hand. She lay there, exhausted, with a wounded wing. Her breath came shallow and hard.

The king admired her liquid beauty. She was an iridescent blue and even her long, wavy hair was blue as a cornflower. Rory held her and spoke gently to her as he sat upon the bank.

"Wake, little nymph. You are safe now, wake," he said.

He hummed as a mother would to her child:

> Little nymph, you can wake,
> In my arms, you are safe,
> I have pulled thee
> From the trout,
> I have saved thee
> From his mouth.

The water-nymph stirred, opening her aquamarine eyes clear as the water.

"Oh, sir," said Rhiannon, "I thank you and owe my life to your kindness. Most men would laugh at a water-nymph like me and enjoy watching her be consumed by a fish, but you are different. There is kindness in your heart."

Rory was enchanted by the little creature and forgot his own warnings to be careful.

"Let me repay you, my lord. Come and relax with me on my barge, for you have been hunting all day and are tired."

Rory's good judgment failed as he was fascinated by this water-nymph. How could she have known that he had been hunting if she were not a witch? Cigfa and her table of delicacies, Branwen and her telling-cards; both were forgotten as Rory descended beneath the enchantment of the seemingly helpless and pitifully seductive Rhiannon.

She had tricked him by appealing to his good nature, knowing that he would help her; knowing that he was of noble birth and would not deny aid to one in distress. And now he was hers. She delighted in this show of power; this triumph over her two older sisters.

Rhiannon chirped a little bird song like a nightingale and there appeared in the brook a chalk-white barge pulled by two giant swans. As if in a trance, Rory forgot about Cymbeline, who was tethered too far away to warn the monarch, and lay down upon the barge covered in swans' feathers. He could not remember ever feeling so at ease, so sleepy. Rhiannon was in his hand as he lay there, gently rocked by the push of the powerful webbed feet of the swans, black and unseen beneath the surface of the stream.

"Rory," Rhiannon whispered.

And when he looked again, the little nymph had become a woman, still blue as a lake, but without her wings. She reached for him and he for her.

"Rhiannon," he whispered, having no idea how he had come to know her name.

Her sisters looked on with envy, seeing that Rhiannon had succeeded in seducing the handsome stranger where they had not. She, of the three, had won his heart. How clever of her to transform herself into a seemingly helpless nymph.

Chapter Five

Rory remembered very little when he awoke. *Had it been a dream? It must have,* he thought, *as swans do not draw barges lined with feathers. And although women come in many shades, aquamarine is not one of them.* Nay, it must have been a dream and he must have been more tired than usual, for he was still in the forest at daybreak of a new morn and not in the castle where he belonged. People would worry about him. They were probably searching for him. He must not alarm them.

The king got up wearily, stretched his long limbs, and walked toward Cymbeline, ever faithful, still tied and waiting for her master. One thing Rory noticed was that his birds were gone – *taken by some animal in the night for food,* he thought. He was lucky, because a human robber would almost certainly have stolen his purse as well and possibly even attacked him while he slept, had he stirred.

The young hunter thought that this turn of luck portended a good day ahead, so he untied the horse and brushed his hair back from his face. With a click of his tongue, they were off toward Caradon Hall, and, hopefully, a hot and hearty breakfast. It was one of the plusses of being king; they brought him food and he was grateful, remembering his humble beginnings.

Two thoughts troubled him, though, and refused to leave his mind, no matter how hard he tried to banish them. *Those two witches.* They had cursed him. Not that he really believed in curses. He put no stock in the stain upon his cheek as marking him for evil. But still, there they were, stuck like honey upon toast in his mind.

The other troubling thought stuck even harder. It was more welded on as the blacksmith welds the hilt of the sword to the blade. *Have I been with that woman, the blue one?* Rory felt that he had, but only in a dream as if he were floating above the scene, observing it as a disinterested party. But he could not be sure.

Nevertheless, Rory resolved to be of good cheer and put on a good face. He approached the castle and trumpets sounded. The people were relieved. The king had returned, hungry as a wolf, but safe and sound, thanks be to God.

Chapter Six

Rhiannon reclined upon the soft floor of the barge, softer than a hay-bed, more luxurious than a queen's bed. Her weight rested upon one hip and one elbow. Her lithe, yet womanly, body a series of rounded curves. She looked at the man next to her and their eyes met. Rory was transfixed. He had seen blue eyes before, but the eyes of the nymph-woman were a jewel-like blue with flecks of yellow, pink, and white, like newborn flowers on an April morn. They were liquid, like the medium which served as this creature's second home.

He looked down at her lips, which were blue – a pale blue leaning toward lavender. As Rory took Rhiannon into his muscular arms, she fell onto her back and he rolled upon her. Without losing her gaze, he slowly, purposefully, lowered his face to hers and touched his mere human lips to hers, which at that moment seemed divine, made of Heaven itself. She responded, let him kiss her, and hungrily kissed him back.

Rory's head seemed light as it did with an excess of mead. He floated above himself, drunk with the pleasure of the softness of this woman's lips; the fresh, watery taste of her mouth; the incredible warmth of her small body, half the size of his, yet so alive, so young, so knowing. He was out of his mind with joy and began to kiss her cheeks and her luscious blue hair, soft as age-old leaves composted upon the forest floor. At one point he stopped, if only for breath, and this lovely creature became a goddess to him as she looked him in the eye and smiled.

She *smiled*.

He went crazy then, grasping her closer, kissing her harder, mad with desire, yet afraid of it as well, as he had never done such a thing and, according to his conscience, never should without the bond of marriage. He wanted to believe that he was under some kind of spell, but deep in his heart he could not deny that he acted with his own free will.

Chapter Seven

Rhiannon slept upon the barge as the swans carried her home. The small, rocky stream grew wider and deeper, releasing itself into a lake in a clearing. The little blue lake was surrounded by three gentle hills; green, sweet-smelling, and idyllic. Upon the hill opposite the stream stood Rhiannon's house – a cottage really; stone-walled with a wood-framed, thatched roof. The roof overhung the tops of the walls like bangs in need of trimming. Moss took residence upon the lower walls that were quite damp. From the wooden plank door, a meandering footpath led to the lake where the sorceress had magically built a dock, now gray with age, to which she moored her wonderful barge.

She felt fine in the early months of her pregnancy, not nauseous like most women. She took advantage of the delightful warm weather to go for walks or rides, asking the first deer she spied if he would oblige her. The creatures were afraid to say *no*. She might turn them to stone or perhaps even worse.

So, she rode, walked, went sailing in her barge, ate well, and grew rounder in the middle. She was happier than words.

Rhiannon could not wait to see the little one growing within her – this prince of royal and magical blood, this work of art that had been her design all along, for she had lived a lonely existence. She was so different from her sisters, who lived in a grand, magnificent castle.

Cigfa and Branwen entertained the crème of magical society on a regular basis. Witches, warlocks, wizards, sprites, changelings, ghosts, ogres, giants, druids, and others unknown to humans came to their parties, and invited the mauve and emerald ladies to theirs. These parties were more than lively as anything could happen with such a group – and it often did. There was always some unexpected costume, a surreal gastronomic treat, a fabulous new pet brought along to show off its various pieces belonging to disparate animals, but now merged seamlessly and quite often with a grotesque look. Imagine the horse-eel or the duck-hound. And no, the duck-hound was not a breed of dog, but a cruel blend of a duck's bill, face and neck attached to the legs, body, and tail of a dog. When it quacked and wagged its tail on demand, the socialites laughed riotously, clapped their hands, and made mental notes to try to top this trick next time.

The lives of the sisters were one long sojourn from party to party, filling their desire for pleasure, company, and entertainment. But such a life left a dark void in Rhiannon's heart. She felt detached, strange, as if she did not fit in. Of course, she *did* fit in as a highly talented sorceress, in particular given her youth. But it bothered her that the parties made her cry, late at night in her room. Was there something wrong with her? Was she the only witch who could not enjoy the natural entertainments of her kind? Rhiannon attended the fêtes less often and at last withdrew altogether. She was not missed. The others regarded her as beautiful to behold, but dull.

Rhiannon had the little cottage built, where she lived alone. At times she walked with Cigfa and Branwen, caught up on the gossip, and stayed in touch, but she preferred this solitary life over that of the vapid socialites. She was not happy. There was something missing, she knew not what, until the birth of her son, her most beloved son, Dylan.

Chapter Eight

She was infatuated with him from birth. Nothing pleased her more than to lie with him in bed. Sometimes, he fell asleep upon her stomach; she gently covered him with a woolen blanket and absorbed each rise and fall of his chest as if it were medicine.

His miniature fingers gripped her pinky and she was in ecstasy. She gazed upon her son as he napped and studied the wee movements of his closed eyelids, wondering what he dreamed about. She could, had she cared, found out, but it just did not matter. What mattered was that her son, the adorable and chubby copy of his father, King Rory, rested in peace and was content. She was content, too, grounded so deeply in motherhood that she knew not how she had existed beforehand. He completed her; he fulfilled her longings. He was hers to nurture, to love, to educate, and to delight in all the days of her life.

She did not mind that he scarce resembled her at all. She regarded his little face, squarish, with the beginnings of the reddish fur that would become hair of fire like that of his father. The eyes, which began as a cobalt blue, gained color to become the warm yellow-green of the hills surrounding her lake. His skin was pale and like that of others born to Albion, but the lad lacked the birthmark that had identified his father as the heir to the throne of Northborough. This difference sat well with Rhiannon, who hoped to keep the child, like herself, unknown and out of society.

Only bad could come of his being recognized, she reasoned, so she concealed the babe from others' view. She breastfed him for the first two years of his life. Her sisters, aunts now, adored him, but feared the fanatical and, to them, unnatural attachment formed by the mother to her son. They knew that one day, although Rhiannon was blind to it, the cottage, the deer-rides, and the barge would not be enough to keep Dylan at home. He would grow to manhood and leave.

At the back of her mind, Cigfa was haunted by the curse she had uttered against the king years ago, when he had rejected her offer to dine with him at her magical table. She realized that the enmity she had condemned him with would be between the king and her own nephew. She did not feel too guilty, though, because she reasoned that this battle between father and son was inevitable, curse or no curse. She could see it coming.

Dylan lived a hidden and protected life in contentment until about the age of seven. He had grown nicely, become tall for his age, and intelligent. His mother taught him his letters, sums, and witchcraft, although the boy never caught on and seemed incapable of replicating a single spell on his own. Rhiannon sighed.

"He's his father's son, all right," she mused, but this deficiency troubled her not.

She wished to see him well, strong, and happy, and it seemed to her that he was all these things. *She* was happy, basking in the glow of her son's rosy cheeks.

It was when he was seven, having read by then many books, that Dylan first asked his mother about his father. The boys in books had fathers, but he did not, did he? Rhiannon had been waiting for that question for years and had come up with an answer calculated toward keeping the lad at home with her into her old age.

"Your father is a bad man, Dylan. He abandoned me as soon as he learned that I was expecting you. He would not marry me. I pleaded with him, son. I said, 'Give the child a name, lord,' but he refused and left me alone, heartbroken and forsaken."

"Why did you call him 'lord,' Mother?" asked the boy.

"I called him 'lord,' son, as all in this kingdom must as he is the king. His name is Rory of Northborough and he lives a soft life of courtly splendor at Caradon Hall. He looked down upon me as a commoner, Dylan, because I am not a princess. He will only marry a princess. He merely ill-used me. I begged him to acknowledge his child, but he coldly and unfeelingly would not.

"So, I asked him to at least, barring marriage, give me a room in the castle, so that I would be near people in my time of need and for him to be able to watch you grow. But he would not take you on as a page, even. All because I do not possess what *he*, his highness, calls *noble blood*. Aaaugh! And so, he left me, but not before calling me names, which your pure young ears ought not to hear, and slapping me so hard across the face that I fell to the ground. I feared for your life, little one! At that point, he dug his spurs into his horse and galloped away. I have not seen him since."

Dylan stared at his mother. Her story stunned him. He felt rage for the first time in his short life. He had been angry, as all children are when they do not get their way, but in his youthful innocence he could not imagine anyone treating his mother – his good, sweet, indulgent mother —with such cruelty.

How could a man be so bad, so base? And that man, of all men, was his *very own father*!

Dylan felt crushed; ground to the dirt. He had dreamt of his father as a brave knight, a strong warrior, a chivalrous soldier. He was away perhaps, fighting in Gaul or the Holy Land, and soon would arrive home. He would live in their warm little cottage and tell Dylan adventure tales by the fire. Such was the image he had stored in his young mind. That was the father he had pieced together from books. So, went his hope – the hope he had held close to his heart before he got up the courage to ask his mother.

But now the image cracked, smoldered, and stank like decaying food. *This vermin, this serpent, this beast!* His father had to treat his mother so? It would be wrong to treat *anyone* so. *And he was the king, of whom men spoke with admiration? He must be quite a deceiver to fool so many into believing that he was a gentleman.* But he knew. He knew the king's dark past – and the king would pay, Dylan resolved. Someday, he would meet this king, Rory, and he would kill that sorry excuse of a human being.

Dylan made a private vow in his room that night. He took three charms that he kept in a wooden box next to the bed. One was a clear stone, found upon the beach, washed smooth by waves and sand; oval in shape. One, the paw of a white rabbit. One, a wand of oak. Rhiannon had found the tree herself; a gnarled and ancient thing, host to a mistletoe vine. She had cut several branches, giving the best one to her son. Eventually, the leaves dried and withered. They turned to dust, but the berries, the white poisonous berries, he had saved them in his box for future use. He knew that such wands as his were rare and treasured by the Druids.

Over these three charms, Dylan vowed to kill his father.

"*In herbis, verbis et lapidibus,*" he said, slicing his index finger with a knife and letting a drop of his blood fall upon each talisman.

There, he had done it. Now all there was to do was grow in stature, strength, and cunning.

Dylan knew that his mother did not want him to leave. He must stay with her for now, comforting and amusing her until the day of revenge. He knew not the day, but felt certain that his heart would tell him when the time arrived.

Book Four

THE GOLDEN KNIGHT

Chapter One

A white mist rose slowly from the tilting field that was sunken into the ground – or, rather, it was surrounded by grassy hills. The people of Northborough, high-born and villein, would sit upon the hill that day to view the jousts and melee of the afternoon. Their monarch, Rory, had proclaimed a tournament for all knights who would come to the field beside Caradon Hall on Midsummer's Day, to celebrate the beginning of his rule. And when the mist uncovered yarrow, daisies, and lupine, there rose, like the sun, the figure of a shining knight upon the horizon. From helmet to spur, his armor was gold as a florin.

People were already gathering on the hillside in order to get a good seat.

"Who is that knight?" they asked one another.

No one knew. He carried the plain white shield of an unproven knight, but there was something menacing about this stranger. The golden knight was registered on the lists.

Ranaulf had been made a knight for his selfless bravery in serving his king. He dressed his liege, King Rory, for the competition. First, he tied on the armor protecting the shins. He closed the gorget around the king's neck, then laced up the armor along his lord's arms, and secured the breastplate and back plates. He belted Rory's sword to his waist. The hilt lay next to his gloved right hand. Ranaulf carried Rory's huge silver helm until the fighting was to begin.

The fields were splashed with the bright colors of silken pavilions where the knights stayed, who had traveled a long distance to Northborough. Their pennons flew atop each pavilion, displaying the knights' arms and mottos. These arms were repeated on their shields, all color-coded so that they could be recognized even when their faces were obscured by their helms. It was a scene as beautiful as a rainbow.

But no one recognized the golden knight. His pavilion flew no pennon. He must have possessed great wealth for such a fine suit of armor. The other knights all wore gray. Armor was costly; it was handmade by tradesmen. In general, only landowners could afford the horses and other trappings of mounted soldiery.

Chapter Two

A rather heavy, tonsured clergyman hurried onto the lists. His dull, brown robe flew behind him.

"What's all this?" demanded Brother Bede, who stopped to catch his breath, winded as he was from running.

"Have you not heard? Then you're the only one," answered a ploughman in the stands.

He was a lean, bony man with intense brown eyes and stringy, dun-colored hair.

"It's the king's celebration tournament and the prize is the hand of his sister, Beatrice the Fair."

Bede mumbled something about understanding why he was kept in the dark.

"Don't you know that the Church has prohibited all such games? People *die*; they are *maimed*!"

"Brother, do not be alarmed," said the ploughman. "The lances and swords have blunted tips. It is only for the delight of the audience that they tilt."

"Perhaps," the monk reasoned, "it will not end in disaster as the last tournament did."

King Malachy had not taken the precaution of requiring blunt weapons and five fine knights had been killed. Brother Bede walked back to the castle, muttering.

"I still do not like the looks of it. I will go to the chapel and begin saying my beads."

As he walked away, the plowman noted the monk's round physique and decided that he was a nervous eater. But he and the other spectators were in a glad mood, for there had been plenty to eat since the reign of Good King Rory and it was pleasant to see the extra flesh on the kindly monk.

"Say a decade for me, Brother, will you?" he called out.

Bede turned his head and nodded assent. He was thinking that his first prayer would be for the king, because he had a sense of foreboding that he could not define.

But he said to the ploughman, "Go with God," and the simple villein wished him the same.

Brother Bede entered the cold, quiet stone church that belonged to the monastery. He knelt at the altar of Saint Wilfrid after whom the church was named. He bowed his head and made the sign of the cross. He began with the Creed, then recited the familiar

Pater noster, qui es in caelis:
Santifictetur nomen tuum:
Adveniat regnum tuum:
Fiat voluntas tua,
Sicut in caelo, et in terra.

"Thy will be done," repeated the monk as he looked up from his beads.

I must have faith, he thought, *that whatever happens is the will of the Father.*

Just then, a gust of wind came through the open window above him, snuffing out one of the altar candles. Bede feared the worst.

Chapter Three

When a trumpet sounded a fanfare, the audience became quiet. The names of the contestants were read from the list as they entered the field in grand splendor. Even their horses wore robes that were color-coordinated to match their magnificent banners and shields. Some wore favors from their ladies – a lily, a sprig of shamrocks, an embroidered handkerchief – tucked into their helms. But more glorious than all the other contestants present was the mysterious golden knight.

As he entered, all eyes fell upon his bright golden scales reflecting the risen sun. His powerful black charger looked invincible. He sought out the king, who rode a handsome white horse, perfectly proportioned but somewhat smaller than the black charger, caparisoned in the red and white robes of the royal arms. Rory's red curls fell from the back of his helm. He clicked its steel visor closed and drew his lance. The fanfare sounded again and the tournament began.

Knight fell upon knight in the colorful melee. They charged at each other, full speed, lances extended. Unhorsed knights fought with swords until one begged for mercy. The winner took the loser's horse and armor, and continued to fight.

After many hours of fighting, the heat was intense and the remaining knights had become exhausted.

Rory had opened his visor when the golden knight approached him. He was about to explain to the mysterious stranger that he – whatever-his-name-was – had won, when the knight charged at the king with full force. Everyone looked on with horror as the stranger's golden arm became a grotesque dragon's head, spitting flames from its horrid mouth. In a second he was upon the king, who had readied his lance, but it was of no use. The dragon-arm set Rory's right arm on fire.

The golden knight stopped his horse and removed his helm. Rory was surprised to see a young man who very much resembled the old sorcerer, Medard.

The golden knight galloped off to the place of honor and shouted, "I, Mesmin, take you, Beatrice, as my prize."

Amazingly, she seemed more than willing to go along. He helped her onto his mount and raced away from Caradon Hall. Beatrice hung on with all her might. She was quite pleased with the outcome of the tournament, but Mesmin was afraid that he would be attacked and followed, so he rode like the wind.

Unknown to others, Beatrice practiced the dark arts herself and had secretly admired Mesmin's father, Medard, when she was growing up in the castle. Now she felt a thrill at being taken by his son. But the audience was shocked and sat for a moment with their mouths agape.

Chapter Four

Ranaulf rushed to Rory's side. The knight pulled off his lord's armor starting with the helm, then the thin plates covering the king's right arm. Rory had lost consciousness, which was a good thing for the pain would have been unbearable. His arm – what was left of it – lay in patches of smoldering skin, bone, and blood. It smelled of burnt flesh, making Ranaulf feel sick, yet it was his job to take care of the king.

Brother Bede ran to the scene and was ready to perform the last rites, but Rory was not dead.

"Quickly!" ordered the cleric. "Bring him to the convent, the sisters will know what to do."

Ranaulf and Sir Leofric of Caradon Hall lifted the king's limp body onto Cymbeline. They tied him securely to the saddle and hurried to the convent, where they arrived a few minutes later.

Mother Milburga opened the oaken door. It creaked upon its rusted iron hinges. The doorway was framed by an elaborate carving of angels looking down at them from above. The lower parts depicted devils jeering at them from below. She had Rory brought to one of the rooms which served as Northborough's hospital.

He was laid upon a crude bed of straw, still unconscious. Mother Milburga, a kind middle-aged woman with a no-nonsense approach to life, asked which of them was to sever the burnt arm, for surely it would become infected. The arm had to be sacrificed to save his lordship's life.

Ranaulf, still nauseous, looked up at Sir Leofric and the less-queasy knight knew that he must perform the unpleasant task. Leofric sliced with his sword and it was done. The prioress called upon two nuns to clean and dress the wound. Fortunately, the burn had sealed off any bleeding. The king would live.

"We will do everything we can," she told Ranaulf and Leofric. "Go, now, and comfort the people. Come and see how he fares on the morrow."

With sadness in their heart, Ranaulf and Leofric left their king and friend, not knowing if they would next see him alive or dead. But he was in good hands and they were needed back on the tilting field. They mounted their horses and sped back.

Chapter Five

Mesmin and Beatrice rode until nightfall. They stopped before a magnificent castle, its white stone walls reflecting the summer sunset. The castle seemed to glow as golden as the knight's armor. Beatrice was transfixed.

"Does it please you?" Mesmin asked.

The young woman smiled and looked into his eyes for the first time.

"Then stay here as my wife."

She sighed. Mesmin was not as good-looking as some of her other suitors had been. His pale eyes seemed mysterious and hard to read, as though his personality could go either way. He tended to overweight, his tights surely *tight*, his cheeks somewhat pudgy. He wore his wild, whitish hair like that of a lion and unlike most men of the time, he was bearded in the Druidic tradition. His lips were full and like rosebuds. Medard, his father, had been thin as a reed, with a wide and wicked mouth. Surely the son had inherited some good features from his mother.

What may have repulsed one princess attracted Beatrice. To her, he was almost cute – as is a puppy of even a fearsome breed. No, he was not Albion's most handsome warlock, but he was in love with her and would do anything to please her. She imagined life with Mesmin as exciting (the fiery arm at the tournament), luxurious (anything she wanted provided for), and ease (the castle and servants within it at her call). But these benefits were merely superficial. She had a personal, malevolent reason for becoming the wife of the young man. As he was the most powerful sorcerer in the land, she planned to use him to achieve the throne for herself. If he came along in the bargain, so be it.

"I will," she said.

They traveled over the drawbridge. As they waited for the portcullis to be opened, Beatrice admired the skilful carvings of vicious dragons in the stone arch above.

"I hoped that you would like it," said Mesmin. "I have watched you many a day in my reflective pool. I have seen you practice spells. The tournament was my chance to win your most lovely hand. Come and see your new home, Wulfgrim Hall."

Beatrice had never seen such splendor. Caradon Hall was drafty and uncomfortable. It had been built, first and foremost, for defense. But this wonderful palace had clear glass windows. The rooms were smaller, more intimate. Flagstone covered the floors; *no more filthy rushes,* she thought. A system of pipes provided running water; brilliant tapestries warmed the walls. Candelabra, not torches, lit the rooms and the corridors, and even though it was state-of-the-art, the place was strong as well. There were double walls on the outside, twelve ramparts, and a donjon tower over one hundred feet high.

Beatrice was delighted. The couple would live in splendor. Mesmin was, too. He had conjured Wulfgrim Hall and everything in it for the maiden of his dreams. He knew that

Beatrice would not fall in love with his stout and crooked body, or his sallow skin and close-set eyes. And he was a knight just by way of magic. He could claim no chivalrous deeds, for he had even conjured his golden armor and midnight-black horse. But he was by far the most powerful sorcerer in Northborough.

There was no more need to hide his identity, so he had his coat-of-arms painted upon the blank shield. Like his father, his arms were *Sable a Dragon rampant Or*. The dragon's fire would remind the citizens of Northborough of his powers.

The couple got married the very next day. Beatrice looked enchanting in a gossamer olive-green gown. She wore a pointed hat with a silken scarf, decorated with moons and stars flowing from the peak. She carried a fragrant bouquet of basil, lavender, coriander, and marjoram. Her handsome face was framed by wavy red hair. She had creamy skin, dotted with fawn-colored freckles and jade-green eyes. A light breeze pressed the gown of the princess softly against her thin, proud frame.

Mesmin called to a huge iron cauldron sitting off in the grass. His flaxen, almost white, hair tossed this way and that in the wind. Flames grew up its sides right away and soon the bubbling sound of cooking could be heard. He incanted some more and then joined his fiancée. They walked together hand in hand.

Their path was strewn with the petals of a thousand flowers. Beatrice and Mesmin stopped beneath a wooden arbor covered with morning glory and sweet pea vines. A satyr had come from Anshan to administer the ancient vows. He spoke in a tongue old as the ocean.

The ceremony complete, the minstrels struck up a merry tune on their lute, harp, and flute. The great black cauldron had finished cooking the wedding feast.

Maidservants carried dishes of roast pheasant, haunch of venison, round of beef, pork sausage, and leg of mutton to the boards. There were casks of the finest wine from across the Narrow Sea. Afterwards the guests enjoyed slices of yellow cheese with Stubbard apples and Bosc pears. The people danced late into the night and thought well of their Lord Mesmin and his Lady Beatrice.

"Such a lovely girl," they said.

But if the guests had to know her thoughts, they would find her ugly as, in her head, Beatrice was already plotting to become queen, with Mesmin as king of Northborough. She meant to end King Rory's rule. It was for this purpose that she had consented to be carried away by him.

Chapter Six

Rory turned over on the straw mattress, wondering where he was. It was a gray day with low misty clouds and no sun. He observed the simplicity of his room, which contained only a bed, a small table, and a carved crucifix on the wall. A young woman walked in with a wooden tray.

She noticed that the king's eyes were open and curtsied, saying, "Forgive me, sire, but you have been asleep for two days and you must be hungry."

Rory went to reach for the tray, but was horrified to find that his right arm was gone. He looked at the girl serving him and sighed in frustration. He thought of how ridiculous he must look, lord of the realm, helpless as a babe lying in a cot. He began to chuckle.

"I must laugh as it is not befitting for a king to cry," he said, noticing her face for the first time.

The white habit of her order enclosed its perfection. Her full, brown eyes and soft, expressive lips were so pleasant to view that he found himself staring. The girl looked away, blushing. She set the tray next to his bed and started to leave.

"Do not go, please. My name is Rory, but you know that already. I do not know yours."

"I am called Clothilde."

"And Clothilde, we are in Saint Bathilde's Convent, is that right? I was brought here after the golden knight set my arm on fire?"

"Yes, milord."

"I wonder at his hostility. Why would he harm me in this way, especially as I was about to congratulate him on his victory in the tournament?"

Rory sat up in bed. He clumsily tried to eat with his left hand, but only succeeded in covering his linen tunic with beef and gravy.

"I'm afraid you'll have to help me with this," he said, smiling at her in a boyish way.

"I will bring new clothes and a chair, milord. It will not take a minute."

Clothilde returned. She helped Rory to remove his soiled garment and put on a new one. The king could no longer button his clothes. He felt helpless, yet buoyant, at being taken care of by this sweet postulant. She sat down and fed him the meal.

"You do not find my birthmark offensive?" he asked.

"Not at all, sire. You are blessed with a comely face."

Against her will, Clothilde found herself falling in love with the king.

It must not be, she thought. *I am just a common girl without a drop of royal blood in my veins. The king is expected to make a clever match – with the daughter of an earl, a baron, or a king. He is to increase the size of his kingdom by choosing wisely and I have nothing at all to offer him. Nothing! Besides, I shall soon take my final vows.*

She picked up the tray and tried to leave, but the king stopped her again. He used his left arm, still large and powerful.

"Clothilde, thank you."

Rory wished that the girl could stay by his side forever.

"It is my duty to serve you, milord."

The postulant walked gracefully away. Rory had fallen totally, hopelessly in love.

Chapter Seven

Beatrice was sitting in the solar with her husband.

"You know, dear, there is no reason why *you* should not be king. You can see how ineffective my brother is. He has repealed the taxes that your father so wisely advised. His court is no longer considered the most resplendent in Albion and how is he to raise an army without taxes? Does he not care if we are attacked by the barbarians across the marches or the greedy devils across the Narrow Sea? And how are knights to prove their bravery? In these incessant tournaments and jousts? What fighting man would not rather earn his golden spurs on the battlefield than at play? Nay, husband, Rory knows not how to secure the happiness of his people. It is time for a new king."

"But, Beatrice, are you not content to live here in our own home? I have tried to give you everything – tapestries, exotic pets, jewelry, minstrels, poets – and I am afraid that I have burnt the king's arm horribly. I just meant to frighten him. Could we not just live our lives in peace?"

"I can see that you have inherited your father's visage, but none of his vision. You are a great sorcerer, though, and you must not waste your powers."

"Sometimes it all seems so *easy*. Other people have to *work* for things," he said.

"Mesmin, if you talk like that again, I shall wonder if you have lost your wits. And it is not true that you have given me everything, for the one thing I desire most is to be queen of Northborough and I need your help. You have *not* gotten me *that*. Now are you with me or not?"

"You know that I am yours and will do anything to please you. What do you suggest, wife?"

"You must kill Rory, of course. But then my elder sister, Catherine, could marry and claim the throne for her husband."

"We don't have to kill her, too, do we?"

"No, my weak husband, but we must make absolutely certain that she is put away for the rest of her life. I do maintain *some* affection for my childhood playmate."

"You have a plan," Mesmin responded with fear, for he really was mild-mannered and uncomfortable with violence.

Why could not his wife be happy in the grandest hall in Northborough? He had not anticipated that she would demand to become queen. The sorcerer suspected that Beatrice, who had no reason to envy anyone, nursed a hidden jealousy in her heart. He hoped that one day she would trust him enough to tell him all her troubles, but for now it was too soon. They were just married.

"Have I a plan, husband? Indeed, I do."

Chapter Eight

It was late summer and the land was bringing forth of its fruits. The peasants worked hard, but with gladness as their stomachs were full and the taxes low. Mothers bought new cloth for kirtles, cloaks, and breeches. Prosperity reigned in Northborough.

Princess Catherine still lived at court. She resembled her sister so much that the two girls could be mistaken for identical twins, but they were not as Catherine was three years older than Beatrice. Both of them had hair like a hearth fire and bewitching green eyes. They were slim, graceful, and educated in the arts of the nobility.

"This needlepoint grows tiresome. On a day such as this, I should be out of doors," she said to her lady-in-waiting, who procured Catherine's hat and large leather glove.

Catherine walked toward the mews behind the castle. She had a special softness in her heart for animals and birds. With them, she was most comfortable. Proper activities of noble ladies bored her terribly. Morrigna was her little merlin falcon. She had been practicing with her on a creance and today, for the first time, she would let her fly freely.

"Good morn, Morrigna," she said, removing the bird's hood.

The falcon sat upon Catherine's outstretched arm. Old Ulric came along to assist the princess and act as valet. He walked through the brush growing at the edge of the meadow and hit the bushes with a long stick. A startled pigeon flew out.

Morrigna called, "bik, bik, bik," and was upon it in a second.

The dogs left to find the prey.

Catherine sat down in the grass and began to plait the Queen Anne's lace. She made a long necklace and held it out to admire. Its beauty lay in the joining of each separate flower to another. Each flower was almost identical. Some wider; some narrower. Some had the deep magenta-black petals in their centers; others did not. Still, the blooms resembled members of a family: similar in looks, but distinct. Joined together, they formed but a delicate bond.

Once her long-lost brother, Rory, had come home to Caradon Hall, she felt complete. She truly loved him and rejoiced in his victory over Medard. Catherine was especially glad because her dreams had been haunted by the wailing of a helpless babe, her brother, lying in the snow only to be torn and eaten by a wolf (so the story went). The dream never left her even after the return of her brother.

Rory, Beatrice, and Catherine were like three Queen Anne's lace flowers. Each so outwardly similar, together they could form a strong ruling family. But now, Beatrice was gone and Catherine felt no connection to life at court. Her sole interest was in nature and its bountiful gifts – plants, trees, birds, and animals. She spent less and less time in the castle, and the longer she spent outdoors with her non-speaking friends, the more she understood them. This connection to living things provided her with the sole real pleasure in her quiet, solitary life.

One of the dogs picked up the dead pigeon. Catherine heartily praised her little hunter.

"We shall have pigeon pie at supper tonight, thanks to your sharp eyes, Morrigna."

It was important to praise falcons-in-training. A newborn fawn stepped tentatively away from the edge of the brush. It had not yet learned to fear humans and walked right up to the princess. Catherine reached over its head and placed the necklace around its neck. The deer seemed to nod its thanks and awkwardly walked away. It stopped before entering the woods and looked Catherine in the eyes. Then it was gone.

Ulric hit the thicket and this time a magpie was startled into the air, but as Catherine watched the birds, she was grabbed from behind by an armed man who carried her to his waiting horse hidden just inside the forest. Another man struck Ulric upon his head and her companion fell senseless to the ground.

Chapter Nine

The two horsemen galloped back to Wulfgrim Hall with their captive. Ulric, they left to die.

Beatrice greeted them.

"Catherine, how good of you to come. It seems ages. But now that we are back together like old times, I want you to stay and never leave my protection."

As she said this, Beatrice made a circling motion with her hand and spider webs spun around her sister's arms. Catherine hid her horror from Beatrice and stood quietly looking at the floor. She knew better than to answer her sister. She had known for years that Beatrice practiced the dark arts and feared her every word.

"I am sorry, Catherine, but I intend to become queen of Northborough. Therefore, you will live out your years in the cold, deep, secret chamber of this hall. You should be grateful that I did not have you killed."

Beatrice's eyes seemed to glow in a horrible way.

The guards took Catherine away and shoved her into a small room deep in the castle. The room had one window, which was iron-barred, and no fireplace. Several candles stood upon the clay floor. A cold, wooden bed lay in one corner.

The massive door of the tiny room slammed shut behind her, Catherine listened to the lock click, fell to the floor, and wept.

How had this happened?

One moment she was making necklaces, falconing with her little merlin and enjoying the outdoors. The next there was this behemoth of a man holding her tightly, lashing her to his smelly horse. And now this cold, depressing room.

Beatrice was imprisoning her, but Catherine had not done anything wrong. She had just been born first – and for that she must live in a stone cell? She had no desire to be queen; to sit upon a throne would be torture. She never wanted to wear a crown. All she wanted was to spend time outdoors with her horse, her falcon, and all of the other animals of the woods and the prairie. There could be no more difficult sentence to bear for someone so enraptured by the natural world.

"I must be strong," she told herself. "I cannot let Beatrice destroy my spirit. She has left me one window after all and for this I am grateful. I shall depend on it for a piece of the outdoor world. I hope that my faithful Ulric is all right and that he is not so foolish as to try to rescue me. He cannot know the strength of my sister's powers, combined with those of that odious husband of hers."

Chapter Ten

While Catherine was being abducted, Rory was recuperating at Saint Bathilde's convent. One day he had a talk with the prioress.

"Good morning, Mother Milburga," Rory said with cheerfulness as he bowed to kiss her hand.

The prioress began to wonder why the king wanted to speak to her. Perhaps the danger of infection had passed and his majesty wanted to go home.

"God's blessings upon you, sire. How is your wound?"

"Healed, Mother, and I credit the gentle care of the young Clothilde who has attended to me. She is a wonder, you know, selflessly serving my food, feeding me, even; dressing my wound, washing my face..."

"Saint Bathilde's is here for that exact purpose, my lord, and our standards are very high. I would expect nothing less from the young postulant."

"Oh, then, uh, you mean that she has not yet entered the sisterhood?"

There was so much hope in Rory's voice that Mother Milburga understood the purpose of the king's visit to her cell.

"Please, Mother, is there some way that Clothilde could leave the sisterhood? I wish to marry her."

The prioress was surprised, but displayed no outward emotion. She pondered the grave implications of the king's intent. There would be trouble if his majesty married a common girl, but she could not disobey her liege.

"We could send an emissary to the Pope. Only he could free her from her preliminary vows. It is fortunate that she has not yet taken her final vows of poverty, chastity, and obedience. That would have been immeasurably more complicated."

"A voyage to Rome would take a long time," Rory mused.

"Yes, my lord, several months, but it is the only way."

"Do you think Clothilde would marry me?"

"I do not know her heart. She does not remember life outside this nunnery and it may be frightening to her to leave our sanctuary. She did not come here because of a vocation. When her parents died, she had nowhere to live, but found her way to our alms-door. It was several days before we realized she was alone. We took her in and she has been happy here."

The scene came rushing back to Mother Milburga's sharp mind.

That day, there was the usual assortment of poor, sick, and unlucky petitioners at the alms-door in back of the convent. One small figure had caught the woman's attention: a waif dressed in the thinnest of rags, with tiny goosebumps covering her emaciated little arms. The girl's big, doe-like eyes dominated her pretty face, but she was suffering from malnutrition. She was too proud to come to the alms-gate for help, but the hunger had won out at last and here she was.

"Child, come here," Mother, who was then called Sister Milburga, called to her.

The shy girl kept her head down and approached the nun who was distributing the leftover food, and some cooked specially for alms, at the gate.

"Dear child, follow me inside."

Sister did not want to embarrass the girl by questioning her in front of others.

"Tell me, what is your name?"

"My name is Clothilde, Sister," the waif had answered.

"And where are your parents?"

"Dead and my brother, too, of the plague. I have eaten everything in the house and what we had saved away in the barn and the root cellar, and now there is no more. I am sorry to take advantage of your charity, Sister, *but I am so hungry!*"

"Dear little flower, that is why we are here, but I cannot allow you to return to an empty house. Stay with us in our community instead and one day you will be a sister like me. Does that interest you, Clothilde?"

The girl had to think for a moment. She was sure that she loved God and Our Lady very much, but she had always dreamt of becoming a mother as she was very nurturing by nature. However, with the rumble in her stomach, she knew that she had to accept the sister's generous offer. So, she agreed and tried with all her might to repay the kindness of the sisters by learning her lessons and prayers well, and by being the perfect postulant. It may not have been her first choice, but she was happy in the little community of nuns.

Now she had been there for so long that the thought of any other life had evaporated like an autumn morning mist – until the moment when she set eyes upon the king and the old stirrings in her heart were re-awakened.

"I can only hope that she will accept me," said Rory. "Please send your envoy without delay. Allow me to provide him with horses and gold for the journey. And, Mother Milburga, if I may?"

"Yes, sire?"

"I have recovered from my wound and wish to return to Caradon Hall. There is so much to do. I need to find this 'golden knight' who has taken my sister, Beatrice, away. I can only hope that she is in no danger herself."

"The whole community and I will pray for you. *Dominus vobiscum.*"

"*Et cum spiritu tuo.*"

Chapter Eleven

Clothilde was afraid. *Marry her? The king must not be thinking clearly*, she thought. His people would *never* accept her as their queen. She had run on tiptoe away from the door of the prioress with Rory's tray. She had set out to feed him his breakfast, but upon finding his cell vacant, looked for her superior. *Perhaps he had recovered and gone home?* But there he was, talking to Mother Milburga with such intent and sincerity.

Clothilde had left the tray in the kitchen. Someone else would have to feed the king. She knelt down upon the flagstone floor of her cell to pray.

"Dearest Lord," she begged, "make me ugly. Make me the ugliest girl in Northborough, so that once his majesty looks upon my face, he loses his illogical desire to make me his wife."

Her eyes, already brimming with tears, fell away from the crucifix above her bed and closed their lids. She sat back, then curled up into a ball. She did not want to be ugly, nor to displease her king – nor, to be honest with herself, to exist apart from him. She knew in her heart that her love for him was as great as his love for her. Thus, the sacrifice. She knew that he would suffer terribly if he were to marry her, so she would try to prevent it, even at the expense of her own happiness.

One thing Clothilde did not know, growing up in the seclusion of the convent, was that Rory had grown up in the peasant household of Julian and Anne of the woods, who had taken him in as a newborn babe. Class mattered not to the king who respected all: noble, merchant, and villein. When he first saw Clothilde, when he felt as if he had wandered for years and finally come home to her, when he felt as if he had thirsted for days and at last come upon a freshwater lake, he did not know if she were peasant or princess nor did he care.

Perhaps he should care as a proper king would, but Rory was somewhat unconventional in his ways, his appearance, and his fortunes, which, to him, had just soared like a hawk on a thermal. The loss of his arm seemed a small price to pay if it were the price of meeting Clothilde.

But she did not know nor understand any of that. Clothilde was a simple, good soul and when her prayer was heard, it was answered. The postulant felt a mountain of pain move across her face. She gasped, bowed her head, and let it fall into her hands.

"Thy will be done," she said and fell to the stone floor.

She felt her face all over with her fingers, trying to imagine what she now looked like and regretting already what she had done.

Book Five

PRINCESS CATHERINE

Chapter One

Ulric remained at the edge of the wood until evening, when he awoke groaning with pain.

"Oh, Lord, help me," he moaned.

The old man turned over. He had acquired the bulk and stiffness of age. He rubbed his hazel eyes and tried to remember where he was, and why his head hurt so much. He saw the trampled grass around him.

Morrigna, the merlin falcon, sat alone atop Catherine's saddle, crying, "Bik, bik, bik?"

"Oh, now it comes back to me."

He turned to get up, but had to lie down again.

"My lady, Catherine, has been abducted. I must inform King Rory at once!"

Ulric forced himself to ignore the ache in his head and stood up. With great difficulty, he mounted the horse. Ulric believed that his master still resided at Saint Bathilde's Convent. He held his mount's reins tightly as the passing landscape seemed to revolve like a spinning wheel, but the horse was intelligent and reliable, and brought Ulric to the convent just before nightfall. The great oaken door creaked open to admit him.

"Please, good mistress, pardon this late hour, but I must speak with his majesty, the king."

Ulric moaned with pain, lost his balance, and swung sideways. Two younger sisters had come to the door to see if they could help. Together, they caught Ulric before he could fall and walked him into a nearby bed. The good man had a gash in his skull caused by the sword of the ruffians. He had also lost a lot of blood.

One girl, Elizabeth, ran to get linen and a bucket of water to bathe the man's wound. Margaret, her companion, stayed with him, speaking softly that all would be well. Ulric attempted speech, but the room darkened for him then went black. He had lost consciousness. Sister Elizabeth, with a plain face, long nose, limbs and fingers, wet the linen strips then wrung them out in her strong hands. She wiped the blood from the old servant's head. Liz-bet, as she was called, saw the cut clearly as Ulric lacked a single hair atop his pate with which to obscure her view.

"We will need to stitch it," she told her comrade, who left the cell to obtain needle, gut-thread, and alcohol – a disinfectant.

Maggie, as Sister Margaret was known, dabbed the cut with wine. The young lass was big of hips and large of heart. She truly cared for those who needed her nursing skills. It took courage to sew into the flesh of this elderly hulk of a man whose wound resembled two oversized lips set in the wrong location. The slash continued to bleed, but not as rapidly. Still, Maggie knew that she had to work fast. She threaded the needle and set her thin lips together in concentration. She had been trained well and sewed the cut closed. After more wine, Liz-bet bandaged Ulric's head. The linen strips had to be wrapped around his head both ways, including under his chin. His face alone was left uncovered and he appeared to sleep peacefully.

Mother Milburga looked in and was pleased with the work her young charges had done. She worried, however, about what the man had tried to say when he arrived –

something about a message for the king. For sure, it was *not* good news.

Chapter Two

Darkness began to overtake the small cell at Wulfgrim Hall. Catherine sat up and clawed the spider webs from her gown.

"I must be strong," she told herself. "My brother, the king, will rescue me."

Then she remembered that he had lost an arm and was in recovery. A great sadness fell upon Catherine.

She crawled over to the array of candles that had been left upon the floor. She had no means with which to light them. As she thought about that, the candles began to glow of their own accord and she became frightened. Whereas a normal flame would dance in shades of persimmon and gold, these eerie candles emitted an ochre-green luminescence almost as if they existed underneath a mossy sea.

"It's my terrible sister and her sorcery again," she exclaimed and, in anger, blew out the candles one by one.

Now she welcomed the darkness; it was a chance to calm down and rest. Catherine climbed into the rustic bed and tried to sleep. However, when sleep is most desired, it often stays just out of reach.

Catherine's thoughts swarmed with olive-yellow candles. Worry for poor Ulric tormented her mind. *Where was Morrigna?*

This night was the first in which the young princess had not changed into a nightgown, washed her face, and brushed out her long, red hair. She missed the routine. At least she could still say her goodnight prayers.

The scamper of a mouse startled her, but mice will come, she reasoned, as she had left her dinner untouched near the door. The mouse was thrilled to find such a bounty and scurried away to bring his relatives. After they had finished every remaining crumb, they began to sing:

"We gather wheat; we gather corn;
Beginning at the dawn of morn,
We put away for the 'morrow
Lest we starve in winter sorrow."

Catherine had never heard mice sing before. Their little voices joined high above them like a choir of angels. She relaxed for a while, listening to her tiny visitors sing their thanks for the meal.

The young lass realized that since she was held in an enchanted castle, it was not surprising that mice could sing. *They must have learned that song from the threshers in the barn.* She smiled at them and clapped her hands softly, so that no one else in her prison would hear.

The mice knew many human songs. Catherine always left part of her dinner for them to share. In return, they sang for her every evening. These songs comforted her and helped her to sleep. The mice-friends probably kept the girl from losing her sanity in the lonely months that would follow, but they could not prevent her from losing health.

The cold, damp cell took its toll on the young woman, who was so used to living outdoors in the sunshine. It did not help that the rations allocated to her were meager and unappetizing. She imagined that she was served what even the dogs that lived underneath the boards refused to eat. Hearing no word from outside, she assumed the worst. *Rory must have died,* she thought. She spent her days looking out of her tiny window and wondering what was going on in Northborough.

The occasional bird flying by was a grand event. All she received was food and a cloak as the cold weather approached: she was given a worn-out blanket. Catherine began to have trouble breathing and then to cough. By autumn, when chilly winds raced through the cell, she coughed deeply without cease.

Chapter Three

When Catherine did not come home that day after going hunting with Morrigna, the castle was in uproar. Knights scoured the nearby woods and the countryside. Rory paced the great hall, trying to imagine what had happened to his sister and her guardian, Ulric.

Then came the news that Ulric was lying wounded at Saint Bathilde's Convent and Rory insisted on traveling there to see the servant. The old man looked as though he would pull through, owing to Liz-bet and Maggie's care. They changed his bandages often, read to him, and never left his side.

A single candle lit the small cell where the old fellow lay. It flickered as Rory walked in, making the girls' silhouettes stretch and move hauntingly upon the stone walls.

"They've taken her, sire," Ulric managed to say, his voice raspy, barely audible.

"Where to, friend?" the king said softly, bending low to Ulric's face, which remained contorted in pain.

"I am sorry, Lord, but I know not. Two brigands there were and they grabbed the princess and tied her to a horse. That was the last thing I remember. I have failed you, sire, and no punishment would be too great for me. You trusted me with her life and I was watching a magpie instead."

The lines of his face grew deeper. His sadness was overwhelming.

"Do not waste your strength on such nonsense, good man. There was obviously more than one of them and they were armed at that. They had planned an ambush. They were certainly *not* gentlemen as no gentleman would treat a lady so. It is not your fault, Ulric, but I am grateful to you for telling me truthfully what you know. Now I must concentrate upon getting Catherine back home and you must concentrate on getting better. Take care of yourself, rest, eat the good sisters' food, and I will see you again as soon as there is news."

"Thank you, sire. It is not my place to say so, but I loved the young lass like a daughter, you know."

"I know, Ulric," said the king. "I know."

Chapter Four

"*Splendidly*, husband. Our plan is working out splendidly," Bea told her spouse.

"Which plan, again, dear?"

"You fool, do not try my patience! You know which plan – the plan to make you king of Northborough," she snapped at him.

"And you its queen, no doubt? That plan?"

Beatrice was ready to strike her husband when she saw the beginnings of a grin turn up the corners of Mesmin's mouth. She relaxed and laughed a little herself.

"Oh, you're teasing me," she said, trying to sound good-natured. In reality, she was impatient and anxious. It was time to move on to the next step and Mesmin always seemed to dawdle.

"You really are beautiful when you're angry," he ventured, hoping to change the subject.

"I know what you are doing, but flattery will get you nowhere as they say. I already know I am beautiful. And cunning. It is *you* who is slow and unattractive."

"Why did you marry me again, dear? I adore it when you are romantic with me."

"Idiot! I wished to live in the finest hall in Albion. I wanted my brother and sister to be jealous, but Rory only thinks about improving the lot of his blessed peasants and Catherine about plants and birds and things. So, let me speak quite frankly, husband. I married you because you are the most powerful sorcerer in the land and you will help me to become queen. Is it so terrible a thing to become king, dear?"

Her voice became sugary near the end.

"Well, it's just that there already *is* a king."

"Silence! Let me get back to the topic at hand. I want you to conjure an army. You are to have knights, foot-soldiers and bowmen. You must not just create this army, but also train it in the ways of siege and battle. The army must have clothes, weapons, and food. I am giving you three months to accomplish this task, Mesmin, and not one day more. That ineffective king still knows not where his sister resides, but he may find out any day. You are to prepare for war, my husband, and in such a way that we cannot lose. You wouldn't want to lose, would you, dear?"

"Oh, no, Beatrice the fair. I would much rather *win*, naturally."

"Then go to work. Three months. Three months from today, we go to war. We must do it before winter sets in."

Mesmin thought it was unnatural for a woman to be so bloodthirsty, but he went along with his wife's wishes. He could not help himself as he loved her. He knew that she did not love him, but maybe if he did as she asked, and she sat regally upon the throne in Caradon Hall, then she could be grateful enough to love him back.

Chapter Five

Mesmin set to work upon the task of building an army. The uniforms were easy. The weapons, too. Food – he was proud of the delicious food he was able to conjure and there was always plenty of it. He invented costumes for the soldiers and the knights. They were very sharp-looking, black tunics over gold tights. The tunics bore the rampant dragon of his father's coat-of-arms. It was easy for Mesmin to conjure up horses and he created the best he could think of. Each one was enormously wide of shoulder and thick of leg. The horses wore blankets matching the uniforms of the soldiers. They were caparisoned in black blankets bordered with golden fringe.

Mesmin himself rode an impressive black charger. His gold armor was part of his costume as well. *Certainly, all these preparations must please Beatrice,* he thought. But one part was going slowly. It was difficult for the young sorcerer to recruit the men, for while he had the power to make weapons from kindling and horses from beetles, banquets from scraps and armor from discarded nails, he could not create men. So, he mounted his horse, Gontamund, and set off to find willing souls.

It was the time of year when the peasants were busiest. The crops were planted, but needed careful tending and protection. The weeds and crows needed to be kept away; the plants needed plenty of water and fertilizer. No one came willingly, but once Mesmin threatened them with setting their arms afire they went along with him. They all knew what had happened to their king and heard rumors that it was the strange young man from Wulfgrim Hall who, as the golden knight, was responsible for that horror.

The army grew slowly. The hottest months of the year arrived, oppressing the people who toiled from sunup to sundown. The flies, gnats, and mosquitoes bit without cease. Mesmin attempted to drill his men. He taught them about battle strategy and told them how to effect a siege. But he also sat with them, evenings, and listened to their stories. Each soldier was a man with a life beyond this conjured-up world of unreality. It seemed to Mesmin that they all wanted to go home to the real world, where their wives nagged, their children whined, and they felt happy and fulfilled.

It was odd, thought the sorcerer, *how they asked for so little from life: just to tend their insignificant little section of the soil and to return to a straw mattress laid upon a filthy floor.* That was it. *That* was contentment. And here he was, living in so grand a castle as to take one's breath away, with a gorgeous wife and a painful, gnawing emptiness inside.

So. he did not hurry with the army project. He began to look forward to drinking wine with his soldiers, singing, and telling tales. Day after day, the camaraderie grew. The soldiers no longer feared the sorcerer, who was generous with food and drink, and acted like a regular fellow. They came to think of him as a friend.

One day, Mesmin was leading a group of his men on a training mission. These missions were perfect excuses for Mesmin to avoid Beatrice's verbal abuse and to enjoy, instead, the genial company of the army. He had become grateful to his

101

wife for her suggestion to build an armed force; how else would he have met such fine young lads?

In fact, he felt that he was a natural leader of men. It seemed to Mesmin that the men were fond of him and he felt affection for them. Over the past two months or so, he had learned their names and those of their family members. He knew which had a shrewish mother-in-law, whose child was sick, whose crops suffered from disease. The sorcerer began to have friendly, even tender, feelings for these men and the thought of sending them to battle, to die for his harping wife, became repugnant to him.

I need a plan, he thought, and set off upon countless 'training missions' to buy time.

This day's mission took the group further than they had gone before. The day was sweltering even before sun-up, so they made sure they carried a good quantity of wine to quench the thirst. For Mesmin, each day now began and ended with the Gaulish brew. His troubles seemed petty while under its most soothing influence.

The group walked their horses up a gently-sloping hill. As they rode down, the vanguard spotted an ancient structure; one of the few remaining triumphal arches that had been left by the Romans. It was not in good shape. The large stones had been worn away by the wind and the rain, yet there it stood. A light went on inside the sorcerer's murky head.

Mesmin remembered learning from his father, Medard, about certain magical arches. These structures had been used to settle questions of legitimacy to the throne. He had an idea – an idea to avoid sending his men into battle against those of King Rory.

Chapter Six

The king clicked his tongue and Cymbeline walked on. His eyes did not focus; his square jaw was set. He had travelled up and down the entire kingdom in search of the lovely Catherine. It was as if she had disappeared from the face of the earth. He felt that she was alive, somewhere, and would not rest until he found her.

Ranaulf, Prosper, and Leofric rode with their liege. Other knights spread out, combing the land even for a dead body. It was an early summer, unusually hot and sticky. The group stopped at a brook to water the horses and replenish their own thirst.

Ranaulf wiped the sweat from his brow. As he did, he noticed a rider approaching the foursome. His heart leapt for joy upon recognizing Giles, the apprentice who, just a lad at the time, had been bullied about by Medard. Giles was a young man now, but he retained the baby-face of his childhood. Still, his eyes seemed strange; other-worldly. They seemed to be older than Giles – like oak leaves that hung onto their branches after autumn had passed, still crumpled and brittle when spring's new buds burst forth, but there was a golden glow about them. His eyes appeared as lit by a candle from within.

"Hail, old friend," shouted Ranaulf and the young man sped his horse to meet with the knights.

Where, he wondered, had he heard that voice before?

The group dismounted and embraced their new member. Ranaulf explained to the others how he had met Giles in the sorcerer's hall and how the two of them had searched for hours for a snake. They knew to look in the long grass of the marsh and, like an omen, a heron stood before them with one end of a serpent in its long bill. The heron stopped swallowing and stared at Giles who was standing still. Ranaulf walked stealthily up to the fowl and sliced the snake in two with his knife. He walked backwards to Giles, keeping his eyes on the heron who seemed to be waiting. When Giles took the snake from the squire and averted his gaze, the heron continued to swallow his prey. It was as if the bird had been hypnotized by the boy. And so it had been. Ranaulf expelled the venom from the serpent and Giles was spared more abuse from his cruel master – for a time at least.

All of a sudden, Ranaulf remembered the apprentice's gift for seeing things that ordinary humans could not. He realized that it could not have been a coincidence that Giles had been riding past just now, but that they were meant to meet again. It was time to call in his favor, to ask the seer's assistance in locating the king's sister.

"Remember, friend, how I had asked to call upon your skills someday, should I be in need of assistance?"

"Yes, sir, I remember and am ready to help you in any way that I can," Giles replied, wiping the sweat off his face.

The heat and the cold both oppressed him greatly, but he was eager to help the man who had taken him under his wing when he felt hopeless and alone.

"You can call me 'sir' now, Giles, but *please* call me Ranaulf instead. We are friends, are we not?"

"Oh, I keep forgetting, sir, uh, I mean, Ranaulf. How can I lend a hand?"

Ranaulf explained to Giles how Catherine had been abducted shortly after Beatrice had run away with Mesmin. Yet after searching everywhere, she could not be found. Now there were rumors that Mesmin was assembling an army, perhaps to attack Rory. And why else?

"I fear she may be used as a hostage," the king put in. "I cannot bear it. She is such a sweet girl and the only remaining member of my family at Caradon Hall besides my mother. You must help me to get her back."

Giles bowed low before his liege.

"We will get her back, sire. Do not worry. I will do everything I can to find her."

As he bent down, wisps of hair fell into his appealing face. He looked so dear, so vulnerable, that the king felt certain that he could trust the sorcerer's former apprentice. He smiled at the young man. A bond was formed between liege and seer. Rory could not help but feel fondness toward him.

Chapter Seven

Mesmin tried to speak clearly and quickly, but was becoming confused. His wife was squinting at him as if it took a phenomenal effort on her part to try and understand her husband's unusual plan. She tilted her head sideways like a bird.

"You mean to say that the arch falls upon the *loser*, dear. It could not fall upon the *winner*."

"No, I'm quite sure, Beatrice, that's how it worked in the ancient contests. I'm not exactly certain yet how to make the arch fall, but I can look it up in one of my father's old books. And when Rory stands there alone, under the arch, the people will mock him; they will find him weak and absurd. They will *demand* that I be crowned king in his place – and not only because of the arch. I know a secret that will surely bring him down."

Beatrice sighed. She felt that her wishy-washy husband was trying to avoid the inevitable war. After all, what king walks away from his throne?

"What's the secret, Mesmin?"

"I learned it from one of my men who had been injured during training. He was staying at Saint Bathilde's Convent. A girl named Clothilde was tending to him. One day an emissary from Rome – from *Rome*, of all places – arrived with the news that she was being excused from her preliminary vows in order to marry the king. The *king*, of all people!"

"Yes, continue," Beatrice nodded.

"But she's ugly, Bea, *ugly* I tell you."

"How so, dear husband? Naturally, she is not of my quality, but there are all types of pulchritude, unappealing to an *experienced* eye as they may be. There's no accounting for taste as they say."

"Her face is not formed properly. One eye is swollen and takes up a large part of her face. The other features lie at unnatural angles. She is difficult to look at, says my soldier. I can only imagine that Rory feels a connection to her, with his port-wine stain and missing arm and all."

"Yes, yes," Beatrice's mind was rushing ahead. "A hideous-looking girl from the nunnery. How wonderful for us. How fortune smiles upon us. And is she common, husband, or noble?"

"My man says that she is not just common, but an orphan found by the sisters at the alms gate. What could Rory be *thinking*?"

"It just goes to show you that he is not fit to rule. His mind is demented. Perhaps if we put it that way to him and to his people, that his reign has been a mistake all along, that the rascal, Ranaulf, made up the whole story that the boy raised in the cottage in the woods was no different from any other peasant child, they would side with us. After all, look at Ranaulf; he has become a knight and friend of the king. I say he made the whole thing up for his own benefit."

"I agree, my lovely bride. Rory cannot be your true brother. How could he be so slow-witted when you are so quick?"

Mesmin was glad that Beatrice accepted the idea of a challenge, so that he and his soldiers need not fight, get injured, and perhaps even die.

"Now we must explain all this to the people in a proclamation. We will issue the challenge to Rory the Imposter. The Arch of Destiny will decide. May it fall upon the rightful ruler of Northborough!"

Mesmin was smiling now, but one little problem had him concerned. He did not let Beatrice know that he had no idea how to make the arch fall upon *him* rather than Rory, for he knew as well as she did that Rory was Good King Malcolm and Queen Aurelia's son. All this was a pretense, an excuse, to cast their leader aside to please his wife.

Well, hopefully, it was not a truly magical arch, he thought. And, hopefully, he would find the spell to make it fall upon himself in time for the contest. His wife was impatient; she wanted to hold the contest as soon as possible. But there was just one other problem. How was he to survive a stone monument falling upon himself? Wouldn't he be crushed to death? *Ah, well, there must be a spell for that, too. But enough worry for now.*

It was time to celebrate the brilliance of the plan – *his* plan, the convincing of his wife, and the avoidance of battle.

Mesmin walked down to the wine-cellar to pick out an especially fine vintage. Then he was off to tell his men the good news.

Book Six

THE ARCH OF DESTINY

Chapter One

It seemed as if the entire population of Northborough had gathered around the stone arch, the one celebrating some ancient classical victory and left by Roman conquerors. It was said that these arches could tell a true king – that they would crumble atop a true king's head. For a true king would walk away unharmed by such an event.

Rory had no choice but to accept the challenge posted by Beatrice. She set out the rules and explained in writing the reasons for issuing the document. The present ruler, said she, could not possibly be the rightful king of the land.

There was the problem with his birthmark, for one. King Malachy had possessed no such birthmark and this ruler had not increased the size of his kingdom by one cubit. He was weak and lazy. The story fabricated by the knight, Ranaulf, then just a squire with massive ambition, well, who could believe such a fanciful tale? Certainly, he had made it up for his own advancement at court, maintained Beatrice. And, finally, in the matter of a wife, Rory had chosen an ugly, common, former postulant to be his queen; to be the people's queen. Was any more proof required?

It was clear, the parchment went on, that Rory was an imposter and needed to be deposed. But rather than spill the blood of the good people of Northborough, the sorcerer, Mesmin, would take up the challenge of the Arch of Destiny along with Rory, should he not be a coward and accept. He whom the arch crushes and is able to walk away unharmed would then be the leader of the people.

Mesmin and Rory both signed the document and a date was set. Beatrice waited with impatience. She grew even more prickly and irritable as the day of reckoning drew near. Soon she would be queen and the effective ruler of the land as her uninterested husband went out riding with his friends, his troops, every day.

Rain oppressed the people. It was a drenching, persistent rain that had already soaked them to the bone as they waited for the contest to start. Beatrice had arranged for Mesmin to go first. *No use waiting around while Rory stood foolishly under an arch!* She trusted nothing to chance. The arch would fall upon her husband, since he had been searching for a spell to make it fall.

Chapter Two

Beatrice nagged her husband without end about researching spells. He had put in minimal effort, always going up to his chamber – a turret room high up in the castle, just like his father's – for a few moments, only to sneak away when the coast was clear to be with his friends. Naturally, he stopped first at the wine cellar.

At last Beatrice locked him inside the room, telling Mesmin that she was not letting him out until he found the proper incantation. She enchanted the door and that was final. So the sorcerer did unearth the long-forgotten verse in a long-forsaken tongue: the formula for a pretender to the throne.

Mesmin found this book, his father's and his grandfather's beforehand, stretching back to when books were first written upon this isle; of secret knowledge guarded with

110

great care and even violence by the Druid priests, inside a wooden box with a clasp lock of iron. The key, he had discovered it among Medard's jewels; it was one of several. Mesmin kept trying them until one worked.

The dusty, plain, unassuming box hosted an amazing treasure; the most powerful book of spells known at the time. Not only that, but the tome itself was encrusted from top to bottom in flawless and perfect-cut emeralds. When the light from the arrow-slit window touched it, the *libris* glowed green and forbidding. The inside of its leather cover was old and patterned like a turtle's back. Mesmin was a bit afraid to open it – understandably so; afraid the book would require something of him in return for opening its font of vast knowledge. But all went well. He searched it dry and uncovered one delicate parchment page which read:

To Be Said to Coax Triumphal Arches of Destiny down upon False Kings.

Mesmin was not kidding himself. He knew that he was *not* the true king; Rory was. It was just a matter of quelling Beatrice's passion, so that she would be pleased with him and leave him alone.

Beatrice was not ready to open the door until the incantation

To Be Said to Walk Unharmed from Underneath Fallen Triumphal Arches of Destiny

was found. She made Mesmin recite the verses one hundred times each to make sure he knew them. By this time, Mesmin was dying of thirst; he craved a drink and the end of all this boring research and recitation.

"*Now* may I come out, dearest wife?" he pleaded. "I know the verses backwards and forwards. Please, have pity!"

"Lock up your book, dear, and you will find the door to your chamber opened. Thank you for finding these things for me and for learning them well. You are a good student as well as magician."

Mesmin delighted in the compliment and clamped shut the aged lock on the book in a hurry. He placed the box back upon its shelf, wiped dusty hands upon his robes, and rushed out. Beatrice was there, beautiful as always. She was grateful and planted a kiss upon his cheek. Mesmin was quite surprised. She was often so angry at him that she could not show affection. *This change of mood was pleasant,* he thought. He kissed her, too, and was off to find his men. They kept drilling, scrimmaging, assessing the land, and spying – just in case. One never knows.

"What do you mean, 'just in case. One never knows'?" she asked. The foul mood was back. "I thought you knew the spell *backwards and forwards.*"

"Dearest one, of course, I do. You have *nothing* at all to worry about except perhaps in choosing a coronation gown. You look so lovely in every color. It must be extremely difficult for you to pick one."

The positive mood returned. Beatrice smiled a little because she knew how attractive she was, but she smiled even more because sweet victory was so, so close. Mesmin had reminded her that she needed a gown and a crown.

Beatrice set her seamstresses to work. She was still young and slender, and they adored the chance to make fancy gowns for her. The goldsmith was ordered to fashion the most dazzling crowns ever seen; to spare no expense, to encrust them with jewels, to line them with velvet, to trim them with ermine. Mesmin would need one, too.

"Gifts for King Rory and his future queen?" the man asked, innocently enough.

She slapped him across the face so hard that he fell to the ground.

"You must be the stupidest man in the kingdom, but you are, at least, a superior artisan. The crowns are to fit the heads of your lord and lady, Mesmin and myself. Have you not heard of the challenge? Now, work quickly! Time is short."

Humiliated, the goldsmith measured his lady's head. He said no more. She promised to send Mesmin to be measured soon and left the workshop still angry and flustered.

Chapter Three

Rory had been meeting with the Knights of the White Hare when a visitor was announced. Ordinarily, no one could interrupt these councils, but upon asking the visitor's name, the king consented to his presence among them. They stood up.

"Giles, you are back! Do you bring good news, friend?" he asked the young man.

"To be honest, sire, the news is mixed – good and bad. Good, I have discovered the whereabouts of your sister. Bad-" he hesitated.

"Speak, lad, we await the news and will bear it bravely."

"The bad news is, lord, that she is held prisoner at Wulfgrim Hall. She lives, just barely, alone in a small, barren cell. She is afflicted by a cough, sire. Beatrice has put a secrecy spell all around the perimeter of the castle, preventing anyone from telling a soul that Catherine abides inside.

"Neither baker nor washer-woman could have told anyone. It was only by *seeing* her that I know. An armed guard stands outside her room. The castle itself, as you know, is heavily guarded. I can tell you where she is, but I cannot say how to rescue her, liege."

"Of course, my good lad, that is the job of our council here. You have done me an invaluable service, Giles – far greater, to be sure, that the slaying of a serpent. May I reward you with a title or gold perhaps?"

"Lord, to serve you is my one desire. I require neither, nor deserve any reward," the cherubic seer spoke to his liege and bowed deeply.

"Giles, do you forget that we are friends? What is this 'sire,' 'lord,' 'liege'? What is this bowing? One does not bow before a friend. Stand up and look here. I wish to give you this chess set as a token of my gratitude, but much more because I long to be rid of it. It was given to me at my coronation party, but the darn thing drives me crazy."

"How so, sire?"

"You meant to say, 'How so, Rory?'"

"Forgive me, my liege, but I find it difficult to address you thus."

"Well, the thing is enchanted. You set it up and the onyx pieces move against the ivory ones. They do battle amongst themselves and you are only meant to watch. Does such a thing interest you, Giles?"

His face lit up; it was to become Giles' favorite possession. He watched it often, amusing others with it as well.

He and Rory embraced and they said their farewells. The council now had other business to which to attend.

Chapter Four

A hush fell upon the knights seated at the table in the headquarters of the Order of the White Hare.

There was a special room set aside for meetings. This room, in the center of Caradon Hall, had new windows. Its stone walls were hung with tapestries depicting the founding of the order about the year four hundred *Anno Domini*. Torches hung from iron brackets blackened by smoke. One book, the *Liber Historia Brittannia*, sat on a shelf. Another shelf held the *Holy Bible*. Before each knight, a cup of mead. But that was all. The room was not pretentious. The sole requirement of its inhabitants was to keep secret the proceedings and always speak the truth while enveloped within its walls.

Now they were faced with the task of freeing the ailing Catherine. They each saw the lines of concern upon her brother's face. Then Prosper asked permission to proceed.

"Speak, friend," the king said.

"If I may be so bold, sire, as to suggest a plan. It may be that tomorrow, the day of the challenge, Wulfgrim Hall is left unguarded. Supposedly, the whole of Northborough will be present near the arch and perhaps the sorcerer and his lady will forget the guard."

It was a brilliant suggestion. Beatrice was so blinded by her lust for power that she had not even considered the necessity of ordering the guard to remain during her absence. However, the knights could not be sure.

"I go myself, then, to…"

"Sire, sire, please," began Leofric. "Um, your, um…"

"All right, all right; I know what you mean. You are trying to say that, missing an arm, I may not be the best choice to storm my enemy's castle and rescue my sister, but you do not wish to offend me. Do not worry. I understand and you are correct. Therefore, I will ask for a volunteer from among you to enter Wulfgrim Hall, to save the princess Catherine."

Each man stood up straight and tall, and drew his sword, raising it over his head.

"I will do it, sire!" they said, all in one eager voice.

"Sit down, lads," said the king. "I know each of you values his own life but little when duty arises. But which of you should I send?"

Ranaulf begged to speak. He was granted permission, while the others sat down.

"I remember a girl, my companion as a toddler in the nursery. She had hair the color of the sunset and chubby, spotted cheeks. She had her dolls and games, I had mine, but I lived in awe of her so fair, so fine. I looked up to her and reverenced her.

"To be honest, I have not seen her in many years, but I cherish the memories I have of growing up in the same castle as such a lovely girl. Let it be me, Rory. Let me go to her."

Rory had been staring at the pattern of the flagstones upon the floor. He wished that it could have been *him*, growing up in the safety of Caradon Hall, but then he thought again. No, it was meant to be that he should be raised apart in the cottage in the forest. He would not trade the delightful, carefree years of his youth for anything. Perhaps he was the lucky one after all. Perhaps he should be grateful, even, for being alive. He pushed the jealousy from his mind and spoke.

"You, Ranaulf, are the one I choose for this mission. Hide in the brush around Wulfgrim Hall tomorrow and watch for the guards to leave. If they stay, you must return here and we will raise an army to attack the castle. If they go, fly to my sister and bring her home. The rest of you will come with me to the site of the challenge. Let us all get a good night's rest, then. We meet at the stables at dawn. This meeting is adjourned."

Chapter Five

The horses were nervous; they pawed the muddy earth and whinnied. Their majestic heads bobbed up and down, and hot breath snorted from their large nostrils. They sensed that something was about to happen.

Rory and his men lined up on one side of the arch. Beatrice and her household waited on the other side. It was a horrible day to be outdoors; the rain soaked everyone to the skin.

It seemed as though the entire kingdom had turned out. Not many could *see* the contest; it was not set up like the tilting field. But they could not stay home and miss this momentous event. Their own beloved king had submitted to a magical challenge and they would not risk hearing the story from their neighbors.

Was the Arch of Destiny real? they thought. *Was it constructed in the Age of the Caesars? Would it actually fall upon the true king? And if he be king, would he really be able to walk away unharmed after literally tons of rock crushed his head? Or was it all a trick set up by Mesmin for his own glory? Who could miss such an event, even in the driving rain?*

Everyone was present – but for the challenger himself. Beatrice fumed, paced, and stomped. She muttered curses under her breath. Then she reminded herself to act as with the air of a queen.

How dare he be late on a day like today, when she was to make him **KING**? Just when she had almost given up on his coming, Mesmin arrived, listing to the right a little in the saddle and singing. He looked up and stopped abruptly. He seemed surprised to see his wife, her entourage, and an immense crowd standing before him. Then he took in the sight of the arch and remembered, dully, why he had come. There was a scathing pain in his head, but then again, when wasn't it there? He pulled a small bottle from his saddle bag and drank. The wine emboldened him and eased the pain.

He smiled at Beatrice and said, a little shakily, "Right, then. Lovely day for a challenge, isn't it?"

If he were not sitting high above her on Gontamund's back, Beatrice would have slapped him. Instead, she reminded herself of her position and forced a smile.

"Yes, husband, it certainly is. Kindly come down and let us begin. These good people have been waiting for you."

Another indulgent smile, this time aimed at the crowds. She was reminding herself to be patient although that was the last emotion she felt. *Beatrice,* she told herself, *act the part and you are halfway there. You must earn these lowlife peasants' respect, for no other reason than there are so many of them.* She affected a haughty pose and waved a perfumed handkerchief in the air. That was better.

Over the din of the rain she read the document aloud, which outlined the rules: he who is left standing after the arch falls on him, from this day forward will be ruler of Northborough. She almost jumped up and down with excitement as she announced that the challenger would go first and he was ready to proceed.

"That is you, Mesmin, dear," she urged him on.

"Can't Rory go first, Beatrice? I'm not ready yet, dear."

"Of course, you are, darling," she cooed, her voice sticky sweet like honey.

She was not sure if he was teasing her or was not ready. *But how could he not be ready? He had memorized the spells; he knew them in his sleep. All he had to do was stand there and recite, and it was done.* She had, after all, done practically everything else for him. *Was he afraid?*

"Just step under the arch. There now, there you go, dear. Go ahead, now. Good, good. All right. Stop. Turn and face us, please."

There was no sound but the plunk of raindrops upon puddles in the ground and the clink when they hit the knights' armor. Otherwise, quiet. Beatrice held her breath. A horse snorted; another neighed. A baby whimpered. But nothing was happening.

"Go on now, dear," Beatrice coaxed her husband, unease settling upon her composure like a blanket. "It is *time*, Mesmin, for you-know-what. Say it now, my beloved."

Again, she tried to smile for the people's benefit, but it turned out ghastly.

Mesmin was concentrating. There were a certain group of words in a particular order that he was to recite at this time. Yes, the ones he had repeated over and over. Those were the words. They floated just out of reach of his thickened skull. The incantation, it was of a different language; a most difficult one. He drew his wand from a pocket and pointed it at the arch above him.

The crowd gasped collectively. Everyone could see that he was concentrating. He made a tremendous effort. He aimed the stick at the center of the arch and mumbled something to himself. Then he stopped, let his arm rest, and looked relieved and happy.

"What was I *thinking*, your highness?" he said to Rory, bowing low to the king. "I have forgotten my manners. How is it that *I*, a lowly magician, presume to go before *you*, lord of the people, in this contest? I apologize to you and beg forgiveness, your majesty."

A flourish of his arm and another bow. Beatrice could not believe her eyes or her ears. This challenge was his idea after all and now he was letting – *letting* – Rory win. That is, if he *does* win and if this structure is truly an Arch of Destiny and not just an old ruin.

Well, we shall see, she thought. *If the arch proclaims Rory the king, then that lazy husband of mine and his good-for-nothing friends will just have to wake up to the reality of war. I will not let my brother win. I will **not**!*

Chapter Six

Rory looked small and insignificant underneath the giant stone structure. He wanted to think, but had no thoughts at all. His mind was blank. He stood, looking quite un-regal in his normal mode of dress. He did not care for finery; he looked much like any other man in the realm, except for his unusually handsome but birth-marked face and lack of a sword-arm. His tunic and leggings were much like those of a villein.

A small girl rushed up to him from the sea of humanity which girded the site. She handed him a rose; a single red rose. He wanted to cry, but would not allow himself that luxury.

How had it come to pass that he stood there? Was his whole life not one of doubts and questioning? Did the people not love him? Why then, was he standing below an arch – one that Mesmin may have just put a spell on to crush and kill him? He felt smothered; it was hard to breathe. Rory felt that he eyed the earth for the last time. He had not prepared for this challenge; there was nothing he could have done. His time had

120

been spent trying to find, and then figuring out, a way to free Catherine.

He felt wounded by his sister Beatrice – if she was even his sister. He wondered sometimes how his two sisters, so similar in appearance, could be so different in character. He did not blame Mesmin, not even for the arm he had lost, because he knew the sorcerer was in love with Beatrice, therefore, willing to do her bidding. Mesmin was nothing like his father except, again, in looks. Medard had been a truly evil man. Mesmin was just a weak one.

Rory went down on one knee, bent his head, and inhaled deeply of the rose's scent. Then he lifted up his head and looked into the little girl's eyes.

He whispered, "Thank you," as he kissed her cheek.

She appeared embarrassed and ran back to her mother, who stood stoically like the others, all watching the king. The child stood pressed up against her mother's legs. Then a bolt of lightning from the black vault above almost blinded them. It was followed by a sharp and deafening crack of thunder. The noise frightened the people; it made the horses strain at their tethers and try to run away.

The lightning bolt had struck the arch. Everyone stood petrified as giant pieces of stone shattered and fell upon the young man kneeling underneath. And then Rory was gone.

Chapter Seven

For a moment, everything went black. Then the king saw a small, hammered bronze door. He seemed to watch himself as in a dream, reaching out and opening it. Then he was outdoors.

It was night-time and he was suspended above the earth, floating like a hummingbird, but without any effort. Slowly, a moonlike glow began to form out of the darkness, like the smoke from a candle's flame. The glowing light came together in front of him. It assumed human form.

The creature wore a translucent grey gown and a silver circlet around her head. Her long, silver hair was in constant motion, swirling around her like hair in a lake, but driven by constant winds. Her eyes frightened Rory when he looked up as she sat upon a moonstone throne. Her eyes were white-grey like the moon and appeared to be *spinning* within their sockets. Rory felt sick to his stomach, but then the creature spoke.

"Do not be afraid, King Rory. You are here only because you are, indeed, a true and noble heir. While you are with me, time on earth stands still. They will know nothing of our visit. I am Norabrock, the Moon's Child."

Rory looked up at her again from his lowered head. He noticed that her young and pretty face contrasted with her silver-grey hair and wrinkled hands.

As if she could read his mind – he had no doubt that she could – she said, "I am as old as Creation, but as young as the phases of the moon. I am reborn every month, but am wrinkled with worry and sorrow for mankind as men want to control their destiny, but they cannot. They make themselves unhappy in their hopeless pursuits. Are you here, King Rory, to change your destiny?"

"As I know not my destiny, I cannot change it, Moon's Child," he said with difficulty, still in awe and afraid.

"Well-answered, King. But have you brought me a present? I love flowers. You know, I have tried to grow them out here, but they always die. I will accept your gift and plant it. Perhaps this lovely, deep red rose will thrive beside my throne, where others have perished."

Rory was too surprised and nervous to resist when the woman's bony, age-spotted hand reached out and took the flower from his grasp. A thorn pierced Rory's skin as she pulled the rose away; a drop of his blood fell. The wind circling the Moon's Child took the droplet and pulled it away from him.

An old stone casket lay beneath the strange woman's throne. This gained a scarlet spot where the droplet fell. At that moment, the lid creaked and slowly began to rise. Filmy grey cobwebs fell away. Rory could see that the casket was carved with devils and dragons torturing the lost souls. His stomach turned; he held his breath.

The lid opened. Inside reclined the skeleton of a man long dead, burdened with the trappings of royalty lain about him. He must have been a warrior-king as most were in the old days. His iron sword and crown, covered in strange runic lettering but rusted and pitted, nestled alongside his bones. Rory looked up uncertainly at Norabrock.

"What is it you want me to do?"

"Take the sword. Hand it to me."

As the Moon's Child touched it, the decaying blade transformed before Rory's eyes, becoming shiny and looking as though new. The hilt, heretofore black as good soil, could now be seen as intricately inscribed with runes of old. Norabrock held out the sword, her palm facing up; the blade pointing downwards and hanging from her outstretched fingers. Rory had not expected this gesture and he took a step back in fear as if he were being attacked.

"Do not step too far, young leader, or you will be crushed by the arch. You are safe only as long as you stay close to me. Again, I tell you, do not be afraid. I am offering you a gift in exchange for your sweet-smelling bloom. I offer you the *Sword de Morte* of King Rotgar of Northborough."

Rory exhaled, but forgot to inhale. He was holding his breath. He realized it, feeling faint, and took in lungs-full of the thin celestial air. He was grasping for something onto which to hold, but there was nothing. Nothing separated him from Rotgar and his weapon.

"I am afraid of your bestowal, lady. Who was this king who lies beneath your feet?"

"He was an infamous tyrant of our land, long, long ago. He was feared across the isle for the brutal slaying and mutilation of his enemies. They have tried to bury his memory along with him, but it is I who has kept it alive. He is your ancestor, lad.

"This sword was forged from a rock that fell from the heavens to your island as witnessed by the king himself. He decided there was a *reason* for that unnatural event and for his having witnessed it. So, he had the blacksmith forge a sword from the rock; the crown as well. He had the Druid priests decorate its handle in mystic inscriptions. Rotgar found that when he used it in battle, the sword had a strange, attractive force for the armor of his foes. They nearly ran up to him to be slain – like lambs to the slaughter. Ha! Killing became terribly easy and the king endeavoured to overtake neighboring lands. He slew without mercy any who opposed him; even women and children. His soldiers took their farms.

"He began to enjoy killing for its own sake; the act of freeing the soul from its earthly confines became pleasurable to him. He used the *Sword de Morte* to slice babies in two, just to hear the sound of their mothers' screams. He severed the arm of one man and the leg of another to see which of the two men would succumb first. He was a fierce man – more devil than human, some say – but he was powerful and enlarged the boundaries of the kingdom. You owe much to him, Rory, and I am offering his sword to you. Take it and become invincible; you could become king of all Albion, rule the world, even, with it in your grasp. For in the world of men, to be good at killing is to be called *great*."

Rory forced himself to look into Norabrock's spinning eyes. He was feeling nauseous, but knew that he must respond to this woman or she would be offended. The last thing he wanted was to offend this woman or spirit – whatever she was.

He stood up straight, swallowed his disgust, and said, "Moon's Child, it is more than generous of you to have preserved me from the Arch of Destiny. I cannot take the *Sword de Morte* as well. I thank you heartily and wish you peace and goodness. May the rose grow and flourish for you."

"And may you, son, accept and find consolation in your destiny upon the earth. Do not have too high an opinion of yourself. You are, after all, descended from Rotgar, here. And look at him now. One day you will look as he does. Different crown, different sword, same bones."

"Yes, it is the fate of *all* men to give up their spirit and be eaten by worms."

"So you think, now."

She replaced the sword within the casket.

Rory was not sure if he had angered her or if it was just time the visit ended, but Norabrock's eyes began to spin faster. The circular wind that blew around her picked up speed and the Moon Child's hair spun sideways and covered her face. The lid of the casket lowered and closed with a dull thud. Rory fell backwards into the nothingness behind him and everything went black. When he opened his eyes again, he saw the brazen door just ahead of him. He lunged forward to open it.

The king appeared before his people. He seemed disoriented, but otherwise fine. Some noticed that the rose was gone and the most observant of them saw that he had a small, round cut on his hand, but he was *fine*. They were ecstatic. A woman draped a purple cloak around his shoulders and kissed him.

"Long live King Rory! Long live the king!" they chanted over and over.

The peasants and merchants, knights and ladies, cried out and their voices filled the rain-washed air. All their doubts were cast aside. The Arch of Destiny had spoken. As they cheered and rejoiced, the king lowered his head and knelt down.

He did not want them to see him cry.

Book Seven

A WEDDING AND A FUNERAL

Chapter One

One man had not witnessed the spectacle of the arch. Sir Ranaulf had hidden himself in the bushes surrounding Wulfgrim Hall to watch the guard. As he hoped, they had all left with the others, so the young man quietly entered the castle and searched for Catherine's room. Before long, he discovered it. The key was suspended from an iron circle hung from a nail in the wall.

It was not difficult to open the cell door. Catherine lay in a heap in the corner of the cold, unlit room. Mice scurried away as Ranaulf looked on.

He wanted to act fast, so he shook himself into action. *Someone could walk in at any moment.* He bent to pick up the young woman whose frame seemed lighter than that of a child. The knight lifted Catherine up into his arms and beheld her face. It was, to him, the face of innocence; the face of an angel. The pretty girl he had known in his youth had become a woman of surpassing beauty, which even starvation and neglect could not tarnish.

Her long red hair, now tangled, but lovely in its fragility, brushed against him as Ranaulf carried her down the main stairs. He had thought ahead and brought a cart, in case the princess could not ride – and he was glad he had. With immense tenderness he lay her down upon a blanket inside the cart. With a single glance he had fallen deeply, totally, and overwhelmingly in love with the former prisoner.

"Click, click, home now," he told his horse.

They rode along as fast as possible, not wanting to jolt Catherine, but not wanting to be discovered.

Fate can be cruel and sometimes brings men to the brink of boundless joy, only to stave off the precipice upon which their happiness stands. Thus it was with Ranaulf who had never fancied a girl, never longed for a woman, but had at long last fallen in love, desperately in love, with a flower destined to wilt before fully opened.

He thought Catherine's pale and sallow skin extraordinary. Memories of their childhood together filled his thoughts. He obsessed about the princess and became her nurse. He imagined that she was someone, like a puzzle piece, who belonged next to him, but was lost for many years. He was glad – no, relieved – that he had rediscovered her.

He removed her shoes. He brushed her long, but tangled and knotty hair. Even that did not wake her. He watched Catherine as she slept, sometimes dabbing her forehead with a wet rag. He ventured to kiss her and still she slept on. He imagined that she might be thirsty, so he filled a cup of water and tilted it toward her slightly open lips.

Catherine began to cough from deep inside her lungs – blood came up. She opened her eyes and saw Ranaulf. For a moment, she smiled peacefully, only to become convulsed with hacking coughs once more.

The young man was afraid. *Was she dying? No, it couldn't be!*

"Catherine, listen to me. You are home again inside Caradon Hall. Everything will be all right. You will get better and you will marry me, will you not?"

"Aye," she whispered, barely audible.

This time when Ranaulf bent down to kiss her, she kissed him back. He put his arms around her and held her tightly against his chest.

But the rescue had come too late. As he embraced her, Ranaulf felt the last air expel from Catherine's deteriorated lungs, never to be filled again with the sweet scent of the outdoors.

She coughed, then became still as a stone. He lifted his body from hers and gazed lovingly at the peaceful smile upon his angel's face. He closed the lids of her beautiful green eyes and kissed her for the last time.

"At least," he said to her, "you suffer no more. Yet I remain here, to live out my days without you as my muse, my guide, my helpmate."

He sat back into the chair beside her bed. A feeling of helplessness engulfed him. He called for the king, who had just arrived back from the ordeal of the arch.

Rory raced to his sister's side, but saw that it was too late to help her. He clenched his fist and screamed in a dreadful voice that echoed ominously throughout the castle.

"NOOOOOOOO!"

Chapter Two

When one door closes, another opens, but for Ranaulf the only door that mattered to him had just slammed shut. He did not care what anyone thought of him. He did not care if they called him a coward. He did not care if they said that he was running away from his liege lord. He cared not if they accused him of shirking his responsibility as a knight.

Queen Aurelia had granted him a boon for saving her son, Rory, from the sorcerer, Medard. Now he would claim it if it pleased her to grant it to him. He asked the queen to be released from the king's service and go away. He did not know where he was going, but felt that he had to get away from this place so littered with remembrances of his love.

Ranaulf felt a nervousness, an anxiety; a deep need to get away. He need not have explained, for the good queen would have granted him whatever he asked for without hesitation. She was sorry to see this friend of her son's go and wished that he had asked for something easier, such as gold or a hereditary title, but she saw his suffering and felt it herself. Catherine was her daughter, after all, and her sorrow was almost greater for Beatrice, whom she held responsible for her death. Queen Aurelia questioned herself relentlessly.

What did I do wrong as her mother? How could I have prevented this tragedy?

She did not know the answers, but blamed herself in part, at least, for the way Beatrice had turned out.

Ranaulf bade goodbye to everyone at Caradon Hall. They were like family to him. His heart was heavy as lead and he felt like crying. He stood near the back at Catherine's funeral and after it was over, slowly rode away, letting his horse set the direction.

Each night he took some of the money he had brought with him and bought food and lodging. After traveling for some days, he arrived at the coast. Here he felt a familiarity, a longing, and understood that he was seeing the same rocky shore that he had viewed from the deck of the *Cormorant* all those years ago. *So I am near home*, he thought. Fadade, his horse, had carried him home.

Chapter Three

Ranaulf dismounted and tied his horse to a tree. As it was autumn, there was little grass to chew, so he gave the faithful beast a generous handful of oats from his saddle bag. Again, he felt nervous and uneasy. He petted Fadade in the hope of calming down.

"There now, lass," he said softly to her. "Your journey's done for today. Eat and rest."

Fadade tossed her head back and Ranaulf stroked her neck from her ears down. He looked into her soft brown eyes. She was a good friend of his. He had felt so alone of late that he had forgotten the loyal Fadade.

He took some bread with him and began to walk along the shore. He removed his shoes so that his toes could sink into the sand. He felt a peaceful restlessness; a feeling that something good was about to happen. As he walked, the birds called, the wind tossed his hair and the sun set in a blaze of crimson.

Ranaulf chewed a piece of the hearty, crusty bread. He looked ahead and saw something lying on the beach. As he got closer, he could see that it was a curraugh: a simple, woven fishing boat. It lay upon its side in the sand. Seaweed clung to it in parts and fanned out from it like mermaids' tresses with the tide. When the knight came upon it, only by chance did he look inside.

Among the shells and the driftwood, he noticed the gleam of metal. The tide was coming in. Each wave reached closer to the boat than the last; soon the craft would be set adrift. The curraugh was an old one, deep brown with age, little holes here and there. How the cup – the pewter cup – had gotten inside it he did not know, but there it was. He reached within and lifted out the enchanted vessel that he had last seen when onboard the *Cormorant*.

He laughed an ironic laugh. Now that he had lost Catherine, had he gained his parents? Is fate so cruel that she, the longing in his soul, was a mere price to pay for regaining the cup? It might be so, for he knew that fate was, indeed, cruel.

Ranaulf sat down and let his legs feel the cool surf as it rinsed them. The curraugh would soon be free to drift out to sea. It was time to decide.

To drink? To return home to parents who, he imagined, had long given him up for dead?

To not drink? What then? Wander along this shore and another, with no aim, no point, in life?

He supposed that seeing the curraugh was an omen: it was there at the precise moment when he would see it; it would soon be gone again.

The knight brushed his hair and the sand from his face. It was windy. It was also a wild and beautiful place. One thing he must do first, he decided. Ranaulf got up and ran the whole distance back to Fadade and gave her the rest of the oats. He spoke softly to her and untied her, petting her and telling her what a good horse she had been. He was certain that he would never see her again. He believed in the power of the cup.

Then he filled his pockets with the rest of his gold and provisions; bread, wine, and cheese. He patted his horse and walked slowly away. He did not want her to follow, but she was busy with the oats. After a few yards, he began to run. He ran to the curraugh, which was just becoming dislodged by the waves. It began to bounce a little; to rock and tilt. It was time to act.

Ranaulf did not want someone to find the cup after he had drunk from it. He knew, from the last time, that it would fall from his hands once its liquid touched his lips. He hoped that by standing as close to the boat as possible, the evil cup would fall back into it and be set adrift into the great, violent sea. Possibly, the little boat would capsize and the cup would lie underneath the waves. But then again, some magical creature would make sure that some hapless human would see it and feel its odd attraction. *How else had it landed within this curraugh?*

Ranaulf wanted to make it difficult for the spirits. His hand shook slightly as he poured a little wine into the vessel. He felt an overwhelming desire to drink of the cup. He exhaled heavily; his head lowered to his hand, his lips touched the rim of the pewter. Hands still shaking, he tasted the wine inside.

He felt the strange, yet familiar, feeling of spinning while being turned inside out. He closed his eyes as he felt himself moving faster and faster, yet staying still. He called out in a pitiful voice; the sound was swallowed up by a vortex of air. The dragon's cup fell from his hands.

Chapter Four

"What do you mean, I may not still want to marry her?"

Rory tried to hide his agitation. After all, he was speaking to someone whom he respected greatly, but it was difficult for him.

He had waited months for the answer from Rome as to whether papal permission had been granted to free Clothilde from her initial vows, so they could wed. He had gone to an expense for the journey that might otherwise have gone to aid the needy of his realm. Rory was always highly conscious of the plight of the less-well-off, with the image of his good and simple parents, Hugh and Anne, constantly before him.

After all this time and money, and now that his request had been so graciously granted, "What possible reason, Mother Milburga, could there be for me to change my mind?" Rory asked, his impatience becoming apparent.

"Your majesty, please calm down. I am sorry, but someone had to tell you and I could not ask another sister. Clothilde has changed in appearance. She is not so fair as she once was, you see."

"No, I do not see at all."

"Your majesty, please. There are sick and wounded here as you know."

"**NO**! I will not lower my voice. How shallow a man do you take me for? Do you know that I am king of Northborough and that I could have chosen any princess, duchess, or heiress for my wife, but that I have not? I have fallen in love with a penniless postulant, with a good soul and soft manner. Do you think I care if her hair has grayed? If her skin has become blotchy? Her hands calloused, her nails broken off? I am hurt, Mother Milburga, that you judge me so harshly."

"No, my liege, I know that you do not measure by appearance alone, but Clothilde was a beautiful girl despite her poverty and now her face has changed. There is a swelling…it has closed off one eye. Her face is covered in warts; her-"

"**Stop**! I have heard rumors, but I do not believe them. I will see for myself. Let me have a room in which to speak to her."

Rory did not like talking to the prioress in that tone, but he was beside himself. He could not control his anger.

Could Clothilde have changed that much? What happened? First Catherine dies, now this.

134

He followed Mother Milburga to Clothilde's cell. She hid her face in her hands in haste. The prioress left and closed the door behind her.

Rory knelt before the girl, who was sitting on the bed.

"What is this people say, my love? Have you changed so much that you could diminish my devotion to you? Uncover your lovely face; let me see it again as I have missed you terribly all this time. If only you could have been next to me during the trial of the arch! But the messenger has returned. You are free of your vows and free, therefore, to leave the convent and become my wife. Please, dearest child, uncover your face that I may be so bold as to kiss it."

Then a horrible fear came upon the king. Perhaps, he wondered, she did not want to marry him. Perhaps she wanted to stay in the comfort and security of Saint Bathilde's. Or perhaps, he thought with a sinking feeling, she considered him ugly and deformed.

His tone changed. He hung his head.

"Oh, I understand. You don't feel for me as I do for you. What is the embrace of a one-armed man? It is nothing. And my face – I have worn this face from birth, but not proudly. I have worn it, moreover, like a hair shirt, like a stone about my neck. This large and unattractive birthmark distinguishes me from all men. People see my birthmark; they do not see the man behind it. They equate my bloodstained cheek with the power of the throne *now*, now that I have survived the plan of Medard, who construed this stain as a mark of evil. I have survived the Arch of Destiny, but bitter is my victory. I would throw away the crown, demolish the throne, bury the orb, and drown the scepter for thy hand, if only thou wouldst give it to me, a former peasant, and you supplicant."

His voice trailed off at the end. His chin fell down to his chest and a tear welled up in his eye. Rory was crushed not by the arch, but by the thought of living his life alone without his beloved.

The pain in his voice pierced Clothilde's heart. She had not known the depth of his love. She had acted with rash judgment and if only her wish could now be reversed!

"My liege, I love you, but I am afraid that I have ruined any chance of our getting married. You are the handsomest of men and the kindest as well, but kings do not marry for love, sire. I prayed that I might become ugly so that you would no longer desire me. I tried to prevent you from suffering the anger of your people for marrying a common girl who calls not a single possession her own. It is against the custom, your majesty. You must marry a princess or a lady, at least. Leave me, please, your majesty, for someone better."

"Your answer is no, then? You will not become my wife?"

Rory's eyebrows were raised; his wide, green eyes filled with unutterable sorrow and disappointment. His full lips were parted in anticipation. All his hopes and dreams rested upon her answer. She pulled her hands from her face and looked Rory in the eye.

"**There, see**! Is it *this* you want to be joined with in holy matrimony?" she cried out.

Tears rained down Clothilde's misshapen cheeks.

"Oh, my poor girl," Rory said and rose up, putting his arm around her.

He felt nothing but pity for her.

"It will be all right," he consoled, kissing her tenderly.

But rather than be comforted, she cried out in pain, covering her face again with her hands. She lowered her head so that he could not see, curling herself into a ball.

He waited for her to calm down. He listened until her breath became slow and regular. She sat upright again, letting her hands fall to her lap. It was the Clothilde he had known before: the postulant who had ministered to him when he had been burned; the girl who had fed him and laughed with him. Rory could not prevent a great smile from forming upon his face as he held up his shield so that she could see herself. She was beautiful beyond description.

Still on his knees, he asked her again.

"Now, Clothilde, that you are freed of your deformity and are freed from your vows, and I love you, will you, I mean, could you find it in your heart to marry me – a man burdened forever with his own deformities?"

Things were happening too fast. She sighed to get more air. She wanted to cry some more, but held it in. She tried to concentrate on what the king was saying, but was mortified that he had seen her the way she used to look.

Will that vision creep back to haunt his dreams?

But he wanted her, she could see that, and she could not bear to make him sad. Clothilde had to acquiesce, but out of joy, too, as she could think of no more thrilling future than with this complex and superb man.

"I love you too, sire, and if you are willing to forego the advantages of a wealthy wife, they I will pledge my troth with thee."

Rory was so relieved that he felt like dancing, but instead sat down next to the girl and was about to kiss her when he hesitated.

"I am afraid that if I kiss you again, you will change in appearance once more," he said with a twinkle in his eye.

"Well, the only way to find out would be to try it, then. Why don't we try it several times, just to see what happens?"

She was just as jovial as he. They were giddy with happiness and the vista of a blissful future together.

"Dearest, let us tell no one but Mother Milburga and Queen Aurelia. Then we shall get married in secret to silence all the critics. We shall tell them the news only after we are man and wife."

"As you wish, sire."

"Please do not call me that! Call me by my Christian name or some other pet name. But can you be ready by tonight?"

"Of course, my dear. I will be here and I will be ready. I bring little with me but my love for you."

"That is all I will ever need, my sweet, and never a thing more."

Chapter Five

The tiny chapel was aglow in candlelight, which revealed the oldest part of the castle, made of unmortared stones. Ecclesiastic tapestries decorated the plain walls. A crucifix, an altar of stone, and a door leading to Rory's chambers completed the scene.

An itinerant priest had lit the candles and spoken to the couple. Rory had met him on his way home from Saint Bathilde's. He had agreed to perform the ceremony in secret, moving on to the next town on his circuit in the morning.

The old priest had a round face, broad nose, and almost bald head. He was a little nervous about joining this special couple in the holy sacrament, but he understood their reasons for secrecy and could see they were truly in love. It was not, after all, the first time that Father Alban had officiated in a clandestine manner.

The priest entered the chapel carrying the Bible. He was followed by Rory and Clothilde, then their witnesses, Sir Leofric and Sir Prosper, Sister Elizabeth and Sister Margaret.

The king wore the tunic of the Order of the White Hare and a red sash. No crown adorned his head in the chapel as he meant it to be the place of God's own sovereignty. His knights were dressed in a similar way. The nuns wore their habits. The bride-to-be carried a bouquet of chrysanthemums, the flower of autumn, picked from the castle garden in haste by her bridesmaids. Rust, gold, and alabaster petals became sparks of flame in the warm candlelight. Clothilde's translucent, embroidered veil covered her head and shoulders; her ivory dress plain but for the pale sash around her thin waist.

Father Alban turned to face the couple.

He asked the king, "Rory, wilt thou take Clothilde, here present, for thy lawful wife, according to the rite of our Holy Mother, the Church?"

"I will."

Clothilde answered the same question. The couple held hands.

Then Father Alban asked the young man to repeat after him, "I, Rory, take thee, Clothilde, for my lawful wife, to have and to hold from this day forward, for better, for worse, for richer, for poorer, in sickness and in health, 'till death do us part."

He asked the same thing of the bride, just with their names reversed.

Then the priest spoke to both of them, saying, "I unite you in marriage, in the name of the Father, and of the Son, and of the Holy Spirit. Amen."

The couple was now wed, based upon a rite derived from ancient Roman law. Rory lifted the veil of his beloved. The couple kissed demurely and exchanged rings. The priest murmured prayers in Latin.

Queen Aurelia had given the young girl her late husband's wedding ring to give to Rory. Malcolm's ring was a thick, heavy band engraved with intricate Celtic designs. She had also given Rory her own engagement ring: a large ruby-and-diamond nestled together in a gold setting. The pear-shaped stones caught the light of the chapel and reflected it all around.

The king had two additional gifts for his bride: a simple golden circlet for her to wear on state occasions and a silver crucifix on a velvet cord to wear around her neck. Clothilde felt ashamed to accept them, but understood that in her new role as queen she must act as a leader of the people.

Rory said to her, "With this ring I thee wed. This gold and silver I thee give; with my body I thee worship and with all my worldly goods I thee endow."

Clothilde was truly touched by the groom's sincerity and humility.

She said to him, "With this ring I thee wed and promise thee my fidelity."

The priest then made the sign of the cross to bless them, saying, "*In nominee Patris, et Filii, et Spiritu Sancti.* Preserve them, O Lord, what Thou hast wrought in us from Thy holy temple, which is in Jerusalem."

There were more prayers in the tongue of the Church, but Clothilde had ceased to hear them. She was watching the prisms of light that the candles were making, through the tears in her eyes.

Now she was a married woman and a queen. *How had this happened to a starving orphan who had taken preliminary vows of poverty, chastity, and obedience?* The only way, she thought, was that her new husband was an extraordinary man and that she was unbelievably lucky to be standing here next to him this marvelous night.

Chapter Six

When he opened his eyes, Ranaulf found himself in a strange place. It reminded him of his first home – or what he could remember of it. The simple structure, wattle-and-daub, was a typical peasants' home as he had seen many times before. It was clean and neat; there were no crumbs on the board. The floor was swept and the bed looked cozy.

One bed, thought the knight. *Only one.* That meant one of his parents had died. Sadness like millstones ground his heart. One parent he would never have the chance to whom to say goodbye.

Something on the mantel caught his attention. It was the set of little wooden soldiers that his father, Hugh, had carved for him. So, his parents had saved his toys all these years! Ranaulf walked up to the fireplace, the center of the modest home. He picked up the soldiers, one after the other, with the reverence due to relics. He longed very much to see his mother and father again. He needed to thank them for bringing him into the world and for loving and caring for him when he was small.

More than anything, he needed to apologize for having drunk from the enchanted cup. He could not even imagine the worry and pain he had caused these good people to suffer. Memories of the wooden soldiers, the names he had made up for them, the battles they had fought, filled his thoughts.

While he was distracted, a young woman walked in from outside, stopping at the threshold. She stared at the strong, handsome knight who was moving the toy soldiers around. She was afraid of this intruder who had snuck so quietly into her home.

Ranaulf heard the rustling of fabric and looked up from his reverie. *She is the image of my mother*, he thought as he gazed upon the lovely young woman in the doorway. The autumn wind picked up her white skirts and whipped them around her legs. She wore a plain white apron. The sun behind caught her daffodil-yellow hair and lit it so that it shone bright as a stained-glass window. She resembled his mother, Matilda, except that his mother wore her hair in braids and was somewhat heavier and rounder in the hips. Could it be that the ghost of his mother lived here awaiting his return?

A chill passed through his frame. He hoped that she was not an avenging ghoul, but a benevolent one. He was afraid to speak to her and a long moment passed before she summoned the courage herself to ask him a question.

"Stranger, what are you doing in my home?"

"I was brought here by the power of a magical cup, which was supposed to bring me home, and although I have never slept in this house, I know it is the home of my dear parents, Maud and Hugh. I recognize these soldiers; my father carved them for me when I was a mere lad. If you are the ghost of my mother, please do not harm me. Tell me what happened to her."

The girl relaxed. She knew that the young man was no stranger, but the brother whom she had never known.

"Please sit down, Ranaulf," she told him, "and have some tea. I will tell you everything you want to know."

She walked in from the threshold. The wind and sun no longer held their power over her and, all of a sudden, she looked like an ordinary human being. Still, she was a beautiful, thin, and graceful creature, with the same features as the mother whom he had hurt so badly by drinking from the pewter cup. He sat down at the small board in one corner of the room and watched her make tea.

"Who are you?" he asked, "and how do you know my name?"

"I am Morag, your younger sister. I was born after you left, but our mother, Maud, died from giving birth to me. Our father raised me by himself. When I was old enough, he told me all about the dragon's cup and how you had, in your innocence, drunk from it and left our family. Our mother was heartbroken, but she was already expecting me and that thought helped her and Hugh through a difficult time. They moved here, to the other side of Albion, to put as great a distance as possible between them and their memories of what happened to you.

"They blamed themselves, never you, for what had happened. You were just a child and could not possibly have understood the significance and power of the cup. Maud, especially, as it was hers, said that she should have gotten rid of it as soon as you were born. But we know now that the cup had a strange attraction to it; no one ever wanted to part with it until something tragic happened.

"So, Maud tossed it into the sea and begged Hugh to build them a new home – this is it. Hugh looked after me as best he could. I grew up learning how to be a farmer. He taught me how to care for crops and livestock, to melt fat into candles and soap, to sew skins for clothing, to cook meat, and to bake bread from our own wheat flour. I learned how to preserve fruit for the winter and to find medicinal and flavorful herbs. I can pluck a chicken and chop wood."

"And our father, Morag?"

"He died last summer, peacefully, in his sleep."

The fates would, therefore, not allow him to console his good parents. The only bed in the room was that of his sister. They were gone, yet the cup had brought him here. This must be his home.

"I am sorry," he said, laying his head down upon the board. "If only I could have come home earlier," he began. "I tried, you know."

Ranaulf told his sister about Captain Brendan and the *Cormorant.*

"After that, I figured that the fates wanted me at Caradon Hall, serving his majesty the king."

The sun was setting and Morag began to prepare supper. The siblings ate together and continued talking well into the night. Ranaulf told his sister all about Catherine and Morag told him about her land and her animals. The candles burned low and the young man made a bed for himself in front of the hearth.

He did not sleep for a long time. His head was too full with thoughts of Maud, Hugh, and Morag. Outside, the night was cold; winter was coming. Should he stay here to help his sister cope? *But then again,* he thought, *she seemed to be doing fine.* She was strong-willed and independent, and while a gracious hostess, she had not asked him to stay on. It would be different if he had come home to his parents. They would want him here.

But Ranaulf could not help but feel that he was imposing upon his lovely and capable sister. She did not seem terribly interested in the details of court life and he was not enthralled with the effect of draught or disease upon her crops. They lived in two different spheres; brother and sister had nothing in common but a set of parents. Both of them carried a lot of guilt: Ranaulf for leaving and Morag blamed herself for her mother's death. Perhaps that was why she had not married. Perhaps she feared the inevitable arrival of babies.

The last red embers in the fireplace glowed for a moment, then turned to black. He made up his mind to leave in the morning.

Book Eight

THE MARSH BATTLE

Chapter One

Beatrice lost no time in upbraiding her husband.

As soon as they reached Wulfgrim Hall, she screeched, "You fool! You idiot! How could you embarrass me in front of the entire kingdom? I stood in the rain in my new gown for *that*? To see Rory confirmed by the arch as the rightful ruler of the land? This whole silly scheme was *your* idea, husband, because you are a coward and afraid of war.

"You play at war day after day with your comrades, Mesmin, but you are afraid to *fight*. Well, now you leave us with no other option. The only way to dethrone that sap and make *me* queen is to kill him and his people. Burn the peasants' fields; sink the merchants' ships!"

"But, dear, the people have done nothing wrong. They will starve if we burn their crops. And the merchants will be unable to bring you things from across the Narrow Sea – the trinkets and luxuries you are so used to."

"Weakling!"

Beatrice threw up her arms in disgust. She spun around, then paced for a while as if trying to calm down.

"The villein will manage to find food or they will die. It is not our affair. And as far as the things I like, you can learn how to conjure them for me, at least for the time being. You had your chance to become king *your* way. But *you* forgot the spell. Ha! I am still mortified by the thought that *we* issued the challenge and lost.

"There I stood in my new gown – what was to be my coronation gown! Has anyone ever been crowned wearing black before? The heavy damask draped so well and the ermine trim was such a nice touch. It was so striking that I hardly needed jewelry, but of course I could not, as queen, fail to wear some well-matched pearls. But I stood there, became drenched to the bone and didn't care, because soon I would be queen. But *no*, you had to forget the words of the incantation!

"You didn't forget where your wine was hidden, did you? Or where to meet your friends? Just your favor to me, you forgot only that. Just the one and only little thing I've asked of you – really asked of you – and you forget it."

Mesmin was worried. He had failed to perform a small part in his own play: he had forgotten his lines. And now he had precipitated a war. He felt in his pockets for the silver flask and gulped down half its contents. What could he say to his wife?

"I'm sorry I failed you, Beatrice. I will make it up to you" he said humbly, looking first at her, then at the floor. "But if it is any consolation to you, your sister, Catherine, is dead."

"Oh," Beatrice uttered, trying to sound happy at the news. "Well, I never wanted her to *die*, you know. She was my sister after all and people always took us for twins. But how did she die, husband?"

When he told her that Catherine had been freed from her cell during the Arch of Destiny competition, Beatrice was ready to have all the guards executed, but Mesmin reminded her that she had given them permission to watch the proceedings. Perhaps moving the prisoner was too much of a shock to her frail, sickly body. Mesmin, as a sorcerer, knew about everything that happened in the kingdom. He was not paying attention during the contest, but had seen the royal family bury the princess outside Caradon Hall.

Chapter Two

The only trouble was that he had also seen the king's wedding, which was supposed to be a secret. Rory had not yet told the people that he and the penniless girl called Clothilde had become man and wife, king and queen of Northborough. He had seen the bride and, somehow, the ugly creature had become pretty again. He knew that Beatrice would be angry and did not want to tell her.

"Mesmin, what are you thinking about? Why are you so quiet?"

She seemed to be able to read his mind. He could not be unnerved by the death of his sister-in-law. *So, what was it?* He was afraid of his wife, but he was also afraid to tell the truth. *Beatrice would hear about it eventually, so it may as well be now*, he thought.

When he told her, she screamed and pulled her hair. She kicked the air and spat on the ground. She wanted very badly to hurt someone, to blame someone, so she threw her sewing scissors at one of the little dogs that spent their days sleeping upon the floor of the solar. It yelped in pain and ran away.

Mesmin was more afraid than he ever had been. His wife was like a fire burning out of control. She lifted up her pin-cushion and was ready to hurl it, but the little dogs had run away from the room. Mesmin wished that he could give her a calming tea. He thought that he could recall the ingredients.

"*This* is your fault, too! Instead of just burning his arm, you should have killed Rory on the day of the tournament. Then none of this would have happened," Beatrice stormed.

"Please, calm down, dear. Screaming won't make it better."

"How can I possibly calm down?" with her voice rising even more. "You want me to *calm down*? I will *calm down* when I am seated upon the throne and giving orders to everyone, not just to you; you hopeless, miserable excuse of a husband!"

"Dear, the servants will hear us quarreling."

"Aren't they used to it by now? And now, some unknown commoner is queen of the land and I, a princess, destined from birth to give orders, am nothing. A nobody. A rural magician's wife. I have the gowns, the jewelry, but no court occasions to wear them to."

Beatrice began to cry. She sat down and cried and cried. Her shoulders heaved up and down with gigantic sobs. She was disappointed. She had schemed so much, worked so hard, for her dream and some peasant maid had snatched it from her reach. *Oh, it was so unfair!*

Mesmin had never seen this strong, wilful woman break down before. He decided to risk going to her (hoping that she was through with throwing things) and knelt down next to her. He put his arms around her.

"There, there now. Everything will be all right. I will raise the army you want. I will conjure the most powerful horses and the best bows, arrows, swords, and spears. I will train my men well. They will have the heaviest, shiniest armor ever made. Do not cry, my dear," he said, wiping the tears from her cheek with a bent finger. "Oh, my dear, *just do not cry!*" he begged, on the verge of tears himself. "If we cannot depose Rory in peace, then we will depose him in war. His days, my sweet lady, are numbered. Now, please, stop crying. It will be all right, you will see."

Chapter Three

The preparations began. Mesmin already had an army, but he made it bigger, more disciplined. The sight of his wife crying motivated him to work at this most unpleasant task of making war, but he took it slowly and tried to do it right. He did not want to fail Beatrice again.

Mesmin could not care less about becoming the king of Northborough. He did not want to order anyone about. He did not want to change policy. He had no desire to rule over others. He just wanted to be left alone with his friends. But for his wife to leave him in peace, he would have to win this war.

It was not easy to recruit soldiers. The men of the kingdom were happy. They were devoted to Rory and would never fight against him, so those men who answered his appeal were malcontents from neighboring lands. They were paid to serve – not a problem for the sorcerer as he had plenty of money.

Mesmin had designed black tunics to wear over the soldiers' armor. His pennons were black and the horses wore black blankets. The trim was all in gold and Medard's rampant dragon was embroidered in gold upon the midnight field. His knights rode the most muscular and strongest horses on the island. His archers possessed the deadliest bows ever made. There was ammunition to spare.

Their leader, moreover, had a plan. He did not want to approach and surround Caradon Hall. That tactic would lead to a siege in which many non-combatants would suffer from lack of food and water. Women and children died first in a siege, and Mesmin's soft heart wanted none of that.

He would draw the king out of his castle instead and engage him in battle. This meant that he had to destroy a few towns, villages, and fields. He would first begin the destruction at the edge of the kingdom and work his way toward the king's residence. Rory would be outraged, form up his men in a hurry and go after the sorcerer, but Mesmin had been preparing for months. He would have a distinct advantage over the hastily-built team.

Mesmin knew that Rory's men would be defending their homeland, whereas he fought with mercenaries who just wanted to be paid. *Well, perhaps they wanted a little rape and pillage as well. So be it.* That was out of his hands. All he needed to do was kill the king and the war would be won.

He did not have to do it himself. He would not fight, but just direct his men. Rory was no coward; he would be riding at the front of his army. The sorcerer had placed signs upon the trees with a drawing of the unmistakable face of the king, in case anyone from outside the country did not know him, saying that a huge reward would go to whoever killed him.

It made his stomach turn; he was very unhappy, so he drank more and more, and more, to not have to think about it. He was ordering the execution of a good man, a just man, to please his wife. She wanted her own brother dead to become queen. Mesmin understood none of this.

Why was she so filled with ambition? With hatred? Hatred enough to wish death upon an innocent man? No, no, it was too much to bear!

He took another swig from an excellent Gaulish fermentation. He would have to set the plan in motion, then step back. The blood would not be upon his hands, at least not technically, but he felt guilty; very guilty. The wine was all that kept him going. It kept the devils away.

Chapter Four

Dylan had seen a sign in the forest. It had promised a reward for slaying the king in the upcoming decisive battle. His heart was aflame. This was his chance. He did not care about monetary rewards as he had every material good he needed. Besides, if he wanted something, he could ask his indulgent mother, Rhiannon.

But he did care about murdering the king. That horrible, thoughtless evil man, who had never come to see him, his son, nor even invited him to the castle. That blackguard who had misused his sweet, loving mother and left her all alone when he found out that she was expecting. And now, that terrible excuse for a human being had gone and married someone else! Oh, yes, he had done it in a clandestine manner and well he should be ashamed!

It should have been my mother next to him in the chapel, not some slip of a girl with no credentials. My mother could live in a castle if she wanted, but she does not care to. She wanted to raise me as a normal boy in our own little cottage, with our own little lake and boat. I have everything here but a father to go hunting and fishing with, and to give me a name. I hate to see my gentle mother gathering firewood for the winter. He should be doing that – or, at least, our servants would if we lived in Caradon Hall.

The king had held a coronation ceremony for Clothilde. *How sweet,* thought Dylan with sarcasm. *All of Northborough knows that she is queen, but now it is winter and still no word of an heir on the way. Perhaps she is barren. It would serve that rascal, Rory, right. He should have married my mother when he had the chance...when she asked him to do the right thing...and he refused. A witch with a son is better than a nun with none. Oh, I am too clever, n'est-ce pas? But I am angry as well. I will not stand by, while others receive the honor of killing the self-indulgent king.*

"I am leaving, Mother, but only temporarily," he told Rhiannon. "I am joining Mesmin's army and we are going to destroy Northborough and Rory, too."

This announcement did not come as a surprise to Rhiannon. After all, her son was growing up. He was a young man and no one had ever hurt him. He considered himself invincible. He had no idea of the horrors of war, where men died from their limbs being cut off or from arrows lodged inside their throats, or from swords which entered their stomach at one end and exited their spinal cord at the other. They died from axes splitting open their brain-cases and from diseased, festering wounds that turned green as cheese mold. Dylan's concept of war, at this point, was clean, chivalrous and honorable.

Rhiannon began to regret having sheltered her son. She had tried to protect him from the world and to keep him from wanting to join it. She had wanted him – her beloved, cherished handsome son – to live at her side. Now he wanted to leave and possibly get himself killed. **NO!** *He must not die!* But she knew that he was old enough to go out on his own and if she tried to make him stay, he would hate her. She needed him to love her, because no one else did.

So, Rhiannon brought Dylan out into the swan boat one cold, bright day. Ice had begun to form along the edges of the lake. It made delicate geometric patterns that cracked as the swans swam through and out into the water.

Rhiannon and her son were silent for a while. Each seemed to know they were about to say goodbye, but there was no more difficult word for two people so attached to one another. Since it was Dylan who was to go away, he spoke first.

"Mother, you know that Mesmin, the sorcerer, has begun a general mobilization. He needs good men, Mother, and wants to depose the king. I have to go with him, but you already know that. You understand that I have to go, don't you? Please, Mother, say you understand me. Please!"

Dylan was almost sobbing and his mother embraced him.

"I have to defend your honor, Mother, for you know it matters not to me which man wears the crown."

He saw the sadness grow in his mother's liquid blue eyes. He did not want to hurt her, but he was getting older, becoming a man. It was inevitable that he would leave some day. This battle was something he had to do.

"I have decided to join up with Mesmin's forces as you know. I will personally slay King Rory, then I will return home to you. You do not need to worry about me. Mesmin possesses the very best weapons and horses. I will seek out the king, whom, I know, I resemble quite closely. I shall surprise him, Mother, and put an end to his life here on earth. Forthwith, I will return home. There is nothing at all to worry about and there is nothing you can do to stop me."

Rhiannon did worry as he was far too young for war and she had lied to him, all these years, about Rory. She had cared for her rescuer; maybe even loved the man. He was a kind and good soul. He did not deserve to die. But Rhiannon had made up the story of his maltreating her in order to keep her son to herself. She knew that she had been selfish, but if Dylan had known that his father was a king, he would have wanted to grow up at court. Rhiannon did not like courts and, besides, she would never have fit in, with her extreme shyness and blue hair and skin.

Now it was too late. She could never explain to Dylan that it was *she* who had seduced the king, not the other way around. Her son would despise her and never return, so she had to let him go.

"I understand your feelings, my son. I will not lecture you about the dangerous mission you are about to undertake. But one thing I can do for you is to give you a weapon that will preserve your life."

As she spoke, Rhiannon put her arm into the frigid water, closed her eyes, and mumbled some words in a different tongue. Then she drew her arms from the lake, holding a large, polished silver shield. Water cascaded from the shield and caught the sunlight, sparkling like diamonds. Dylan sat back in the boat, amazed at the sight.

"This is for you, Dylan," his mother began. "This shield has lived for many years in this lake. It is what has protected you from harm as you explored the woods and swam the waters. Here, touch it."

The lad reached out and touched the shield. It was cold as ice and just as smooth. Water dripped from it. The shield had been polished by water nymphs. It could have been called a *mirror*, but it was no ordinary mirror.

"Do you see yourself reflected within the mirror, son?" she asked.

"Yes, Mother, I do."

Dylan spied a young man, strong and tall, with yellow-green eyes and fiery-red hair that brushed up against his shoulders, which were like ledges, wide and stable.

"While other mirrors are for gazing at oneself, Hafgan will reflect back onto its giver. What I mean, son, is that if someone should strike you, hold up your shield to them and the blow will fall instead upon its giver. Your injury will disappear. Do you understand, Dylan? Do you see how to use it?"

"I do, Mother."

He was contemplating the immense worth of her gift. It made him quiet and thoughtful. How kind his mother was!

"Here, take it, then."

The boy took Hafgan from his mother. It was lighter than expected. He could hold it in his left hand with ease, while brandishing a sword in his right hand. There was an intricate design around its circular border and ancient lettering inscribed on the unpolished back. A bar was welded into the back to hold the shield. He did not know what the letters meant and did not want to appear stupid by asking his mother.

It was a very special gift. He knew why she had given it to him. Not that she doubted his ability, but because she wanted him to come back home alive.

"Thank you, Mother. I mean it. Thank you so much. It is a most generous present."

"You are welcome, son, and good luck to you. May it bring you home safely."

Rhiannon held Dylan close.

He packed his things and left early in the morning. Snow was coming; the deep grey clouds warned him. It was best to set out.

Chapter Five

Rory paced the width of the small room where the Order of the White Hare met. At each turn, his tunic flew around behind him. The knights were as angry as their king; they were anxious to right the wrongs inflicted upon the people.

"Sire, they have burned the peasants' fields. There will be widespread starvation this winter," Sir Leofric told Rory, slamming his cup upon the board.

"Mesmin's men are stealing anything of value. Even the churches' sacred vessels are not safe. Moreover, sire, they are taking advantage of the women," added Sir Prosper.

"The devils are destroying the towns. They have ruined the marketplace and spilled innocent blood," another knight added. "What is to be done?"

"We cannot allow the destruction of the life and property of our good people to go on," the king said with great sadness, looking down. "I am left with no option but to meet the enemy on the battlefield. I know what this invasion means – even more people will die: soldiers, women, the young, the aged. But if we do nothing, the land will be laid waste and there will be no happiness for the people under Mesmin's rule. He and his wife seek only pleasure and power for themselves; they care not for the villein. With a heavy heart, I order you to prepare for battle. We ride to meet the enemy at dawn. Let all the young men know – **to arms**! Let the church bells ring out – **to arms**!

"So, Mesmin, you did not defeat me with your magical arch. Now we shall meet in one final, decisive battle. Go now, comrades, and prepare for the day of trial. Prepare thy weapons, prepare thy horses, prepare thy souls. It will be an ugly day, but we must not cringe from the precipice. It is our duty to defend our homeland. **For Northborough, lads!**"

"**For Northborough!**" they echoed.

Chapter Six

Rory was deeply troubled by the prospect of war. He explained everything to Clothilde, who listened with widened eyes. She understood that as the king, her husband must lead his army. He was its general. She assured him of her constant prayers. She also promised to work at the hospital of Saint Bathilde's to care for the wounded and the dying. They kissed with great tenderness. However, there was much yet to do for the young ruler.

Mesmin's men drank heartily and feasted into the night and early morning, when their bonfires died down. They were enjoying the spoils of war; a war they were winning. But they had yet to engage the enemy. Rory found his confessor and, like many of his men, sought on his knees to wash clean his soul before, perhaps, releasing it upon the heavens the next day. Young men and older ones, hearing the church bells, did the same. Everyone in Northborough talked of the invasion. No one slept much that night.

The people frantically tried to defend their homes. Some came to the shelter of Caradon Hall and were accepted inside. Others gathered whatever weapons they could find: swords, axes, daggers, kitchen knives, clubs, scythes. The fortunate ones had bows and arrows. The men dressed carefully, although the common people lacked chain mail and armor. Some had head coverings or chest protectors made from *cuir bouilli* or boiled leather. It was better than nothing. Over their bodies went tunic and hose.

Long sharpened stakes were kept for use during war. These were brought out. Men secured last kisses from their wives and most brought along with them a token such as a piece of embroidery or a pressed flower.

It was cold, bitter cold, that night. They hoped that the next day's sun would add warmth to their bones. After all, they would be outdoors. They caught a few hours of sleep and walked or rode to the castle in the morning.

Chapter Seven

Dark, heavy clouds obscured the morning sun. Snowflakes descended lazily upon the armies, dusting everything white. Rory rode Cymbeline at the head of his army. His knights followed, carrying the red and white banner of the king. The infantry walked behind, quiet and solemn, pondering their fate. These men, farmers for the most part, wore stout boots as the ground was frozen.

The army continued forward. They headed toward an open area where they hoped to lead the enemy. At this distance of three arrow shots, the two sides faced each other. No one spoke. There was not a sound. Then Mesmin swallowed hard. He regretted this moment more than any other in his life, but he went ahead for his wife whom he loved.

He forced out the words, "**Now, strike!**"

The sorcerer quenched his dry and burning throat with a flask. Right away, his archers sprayed arrows upon Rory's men. The battle began. The king's men hurled arrows back to Mesmin's side. And so it went.

A rider approached the defenders. It was evident that he had ridden hard; his horse was exhausted and foaming at the mouth. Ranaulf flew off his mount and ran toward the king. Fadade collapsed in a heap where the knight left her.

"Sire," he said, bowing deeply.

"Old friend," Rory managed to say, but tears welled up in his eyes and he was afraid to look up.

160

He embraced Ranaulf heartily, slapping him on the back. When their eyes met, Rory tried to smile, but Ranaulf could see that the young leader was under tremendous stress. It was a sad smile.

"You've come back to us," said the king, who was happy to see him.

"I will tell you about it tonight, my lord. I was on my way back and as I got nearer, I heard of Mesmin's attack. I flew here upon my poor horse, who I am afraid will perish, but I am here to help."

"Thank you for returning to us, loyal friend. Let us be at our task."

Ranaulf no longer had a mount, so he ran like a madman at the sorcerer's men. The Mermaid's Curse cut through them and many fell at the knight's feet.

After the initial surge of arrows, Mesmin ordered his cavalry forward. However, these magnificent men and horses, gorgeously costumed and caparisoned, were too heavy for the marshy ground that had been hidden by the cover of snow. They plunged right in, becoming mired in the muck.

Rory's foot soldiers and light horses rode easily over the marsh. The very lily pads seemed to support them. Mesmin's black-and-gold clad mercenaries were slaughtered. The king's army advanced and victory appeared certain. The snowy marsh had provided an opportunity for the rag-tag army to triumph. But is there ever triumph in war? Always it brings death, destruction, disease, and horror.

Rory felt no sense of triumph; just an ease of the anxiety under which he had labored. At least he had led Mesmin's army into a trap and this battle would be their last. It would not go on and on, but one day of killing was enough for the kindly young leader.

Both sides engaged in hand-to-hand fighting. The swords, daggers, and irregular weapons of the peasantry met with the mightier arms of the mercenaries, but these lacked the zeal of those defending their own homes and families. The battle became quieter and quieter. The king's forces had won the day.

Chapter Eight

One of Mesmin's men had been watching the king. He moved along the flank and around the edge of the battlefield to get close to the leader. He walked with the stealth of a cat and, dressed in black, blended into the background. Slowly, deliberately, he made his way toward Rory. He waited for the moment when the king was alone, then he appeared from under the cover of snow.

Rory turned swiftly to face the soldier. He was as dark as the bloodied mud below, from his black helmet to his boots. Quick as an eagle, the king swung his sword around to thrust it into the attacker's side, just where the warrior's armor ceased to protect his stomach. The lad screamed in pain and staggered a few steps. He gathered enough strength to shine his silver shield onto the king, then fell senseless upon his back.

Rory moaned in pain. He felt a steel blade enter his side through his ribs, yet his attacker lay upon the ground. *What sort of magic was this?*

The king stepped in an uneven circle, trying to discern who had struck him, although it did not matter as he felt that he was dying. The pain was unbearable, but there was no one around him; just the dull descent of snow. He staggered, scarlet blood flowing profusely from his side. The king's body fell with a thud to the frozen ground.

162

"Don't look any further, Rory. It was my shield's power that brought you down. Hafgan has the ability to project an injury to its owner upon someone else," the owner of the shield said with a sneer. "Not that you could look any further if you wanted to – **ha!**"

The revenge upon his mother's honor tasted so sweet.

"And you – thoughtless, insensitive excuse for a man that you are – deserve to die by Hafgan's rage!"

The mysterious attacker sat up. The wound in his side closed before their eyes. His flesh made whole, the lad stood up and looked down with great haughtiness upon the pathetic king, who lay upon the ground barely conscious.

"Please, soldier, tell me who you are and why you hate me so much. And tell me quickly as I feel the life drain from my limbs."

The stranger lifted the helm from his head and Rory stared at the very young soldier in whose coarse, long red hair and yellow-green eyes he saw himself.

"**NO!**" he exclaimed without thinking.

"Yes, Father. It is your son, Dylan. I know that you hoped never to lay eyes upon me, but here I am nevertheless."

"What do you mean?"

"My mother, Rhiannon, told me about how you left her when you found out that she was expecting me and how you refused to marry her, or even allow her a room at court. You are a cruel, devious, unchivalrous man, who is unfit to rule this kingdom. There is nothing left for you but death and you will die lying in a muddy swamp. Your corpse will be no different from that of hundreds of others. It will decay, rot, and become food for the worms. And you will be forgotten. Soon you will be forgotten."

Dylan did not even notice that the king was crying. He had laid down his sword and looked up at the boy with the tenderest of gazes.

"Son," he said, "come to me."

Dylan saw that he was in no danger, so he sat down next to Rory.

"Why did you call me that?" the lad wondered.

"Son?"

"Yes."

"Well, that is what you are. I remember now, your most lovely mother. She and her sisters had a contest to see which one would win my favor. First, Cigfa tried to tempt me with a table of sweets. I had been riding all day and I was tired and hungry. Your Aunt Cigfa looked lovely, but I was wary of her and refused her offer. She cursed me. She put enmity between myself and my first-born son. That would be you. Then your Aunt Branwen tempted me with seeing my future. She, too, was lovely, but I had no desire to learn what I had no business knowing, so I refused her as well. Your mother was more clever. She posed as a water nymph about to be eaten by a trout. I felt sorry for her and saved her. She became a woman again and you, son, are the result of our union."

"But you wouldn't marry her."

"Dylan, she never told me that she was expecting a child. I never even knew I had a son. If I did, I would have married Rhiannon and you would have been raised a prince. I am *so* sorry, son. Now I am married to someone whom I love so dearly that I would never desire to hurt her, yet Clothilde will be hurt deeply when she hears of your paternity."

Dylan seemed shocked. He did not understand what the king was saying, but it was a possible explanation for Rory's complete lack of interest in him.

"Son, come to me," the king uttered in a weakening voice. "Call my loyal knight, Ranaulf."

Dylan called out and sat down beside this self-assured, quiet man who had become so sad. Rory reached for him with his left hand and hugged him close. Reluctantly at first, but then heartily, Dylan hugged his dying father. Now the only sound was their weeping as snowflakes continued to cover the scene.

"I am so sorry, son, not to have watched you grow up."

"And I am sorry, Father, for harboring hatred against you my whole life. I believed what my mother told me, when everyone else said only good things about you. It did not make any sense, but it was all I knew. I just thought that the others did not know my mother as I did."

"It's all right, my son. I am glad that I have an heir and that he wears no crimson birthmark."

"Did you say *an heir*, father?"

Sir Ranaulf walked steadily up to the king, his sword drawn and ready. He did not know if the king were in any danger or not, but he assessed the situation and understood that the black-clad boy was Rory's son, although the king had never mentioned a son before.

"Ranaulf, be thou our witness. Upon my death," he gasped, "I name my son, Dylan, to succeed me as king of Northborough. Do you understand, old friend?"

"Yes, sire. It will be done as you say. I will write it down. But the queen, Clothilde?"

"It may break her heart, but what can I do? The boy is my son. He is a good lad, you can see that, and Clothilde will come to love him, I am sure. He will explain to you later how he came to be."

The king's eyes were beginning to close. He sighed from deep within his chest.

"Take...the shield...and throw it...far into...the sea, where it...can harm no one else...with its magic."

The king spoke no more. He had taken his last breath.

Ranaulf asked Dylan to take an oath to defend Northborough with his life and to rule well, and with wisdom. He did so. It was the beginning of the rule of King Dylan of the kingdom of Northborough on the island of Albion. It was also his father's birthday.

Rory lay in a pool of red blood upon the white snow. It was the boy's own doing and he was torn to pieces by guilt. He had not set out to become king, but to avenge his mother's wrong. He sobbed over the body of his father.

"I wish that I had known him as others did," he mused.

"You should know this," said Ranaulf, "He was a man beloved by his people, who always did his best for them."

"And so shall I, Sir Ranaulf. So shall I."

The End

About the Author

Renee Kenny was born in Chicago. She received a Bachelor of Arts in Economics from the University of Notre Dame and a Master's degree in Business Administration from the University of Chicago. She has worked as an odd lot trader at Harris Bank, then as a EuroDollar futures and short bill trader at Lloyd's Bank in New York City. She later served as portfolio manager for the City of New York's pension fund, managing socially-responsible and real estate investments.

Renee attained certifications in teaching history and elementary education. She has served as an assistant teacher in a school for special needs children. At present Renee works as an assistant librarian in an independent school in New Jersey and she teaches French Cooking and Arts and Crafts in the summer-time.

Renee's first venture as an author was with a short story titled *King James and the Peasant Lad*, which has been published in *Highlights for Children*. A poem titled *No Angel* was also published in *Working Document,* a literary magazine of the University of Chicago. *The Tales of Northborough* is her first book-length novel and the first volume of a trilogy.

Made in the USA
Lexington, KY
18 September 2018